SHIPMENT 1

Paging Dr. Right by Stella Bagwell
Her Best Man by Crystal Green
I Do! I Do! by Pamela Toth
A Family for the Holidays by Victoria Pade
A Cowboy Under Her Tree by Allison Leigh
Stranded with the Groom by Christine Rimmer

SHIPMENT 2

All He Ever Wanted by Allison Leigh
Prescription: Love by Pamela Toth
Their Unexpected Family by Judy Duarte
Cabin Fever by Karen Rose Smith
Million-Dollar Makeover by Cheryl St.John
McFarlane's Perfect Bride by Christine Rimmer

SHIPMENT 3

Taming the Montana Millionaire by Teresa Southwick
From Doctor...to Daddy by Karen Rose Smith
When the Cowboy Said "I Do" by Crystal Green
Thunder Canyon Homecoming by Brenda Harlen
A Thunder Canyon Christmas by RaeAnne Thayne
Resisting Mr. Tall, Dark & Texan by Christine Rimmer
The Baby Wore a Badge by Marie Ferrarella

SHIPMENT 4

His Country Cinderella by Karen Rose Smith
The Hard-to-Get Cowboy by Crystal Green
A Maverick for Christmas by Leanne Banks
Her Montana Christmas Groom by Teresa Southwick
The Bounty Hunter by Cheryl St.John
The Guardian by Elizabeth Lane

TAMING THE MONTANA
MILLIONAIRE

TERESA SOUTHWICK

HARLEQUIN® MONTANA MAVERICKS

Special thanks and acknowledgment are given
to Teresa Southwick for her contribution to the
Montana Mavericks series.

ISBN-13: 978-0-373-41814-5

Taming the Montana Millionaire

Recycling programs
for this product may
not exist in your area.

Printed in U.S.A.

Teresa Southwick lives with her husband in Las Vegas, the city that reinvents itself every day. An avid fan of romance novels, she is delighted to be living out her dream of writing for Harlequin.

To Christine Rimmer,
who gave us a fantastic start to this series.
Thanks for the plotting, fun and friendship.

Chapter One

She needed another challenge like she needed a sharp stick in the eye.

Haley Anderson was trying to get this small, dingy storefront space whipped into shape to house the teen mentoring program she called ROOTS. It had to be a place where kids would actually want to hang out. She'd hoped it would be ready to open up when the school year ended, but it was already the first of August and she hadn't secured the lease until the end of July. Now the real work started.

The empty area needed furniture, games, a TV, DVD player and probably a computer.

But she didn't think bringing in any of that while the walls needed a makeover was prudent.

She'd only had time to paint the one that faced Thunder Canyon's Main Street, a background for the mural she was in the process of doing. It was the first thing teenagers would see when they peeked in the window. She wanted warm, empathetic, inviting images. Since she was taking a chance with community donations to open ROOTS, why not amp up the pressure factor with her first, very public art project?

As if all of that wasn't challenge enough, she was a full-time waitress at The Hitching Post, the bar and grill just down the street. Although her brother and sister had part-time summer jobs at Thunder Canyon Resort, she was the main breadwinner of the family. It was the kind of thing that built character, or so she'd been told. From her perspective, she had enough character for a small but determined army.

And now she was staring at yet another challenge. He was still outside. The guy who'd walked all over her tender heart that summer after high school graduation, just before her life really fell apart—correction, before she really started building character.

Marlon Cates. MC. Major Crush. But that was so yesterday. Now the MC stood for major caution.

There was nothing wrong with him standing outside—except it was looking like he planned to come inside. But maybe she was borrowing trouble. Maybe he'd walk on by.

That hope disappeared in a poof when he noticed her watching, lifted his hand and smiled. The grin got to her like nothing else, probably because it was fueled by that wicked twinkle in his eyes. It was the down payment on flirtation and fun and made her heart beat faster even though she knew he was a player. He didn't live in Thunder Canyon now, but he still had family here. Every couple of months he showed up at The Hitching Post and women flocked to him like compulsive gamblers to a deck of cards.

He never left with the same woman twice. Her heart knew better and shouldn't have beaten faster as he opened the door and walked inside, but it did. Apparently her heart had a mind of its own. When he pushed the door open, the bell above dinged. She hoped it covered the sound of her groan.

"Hi, Haley."

"Marlon."

He was six feet of long legs, lean muscle and broad shoulders. In worn jeans and a black, chest-hugging T-shirt, he looked every inch the bad boy of his high school and college days. His brown eyes glittered with reckless promises and the short dark hair was meticulously mussed. His jaw was shadowed with sexy scruff. She told herself it would rub her face raw if they kissed, but her one personal experience with him hadn't been long enough to rub anything raw except stirred-up yearnings.

Still, a part of her was willing to risk a close encounter with scruff and she planned to choke that part of her into submission. Along with the part of her that desperately wished she wasn't in old, torn, paint-splattered jeans and her brother's too large T-shirt. She also wished her straight brown hair wasn't twisted up off her neck and held with a clip that made it stand out like feathers from a freaked out turkey.

Marlon moved closer and glanced at the mural she'd sketched of kids, computers, books and sports. She was in the process of painting in the lines, but put her brush down on the small rusty metal table she'd brought from home for her art supplies.

"That's impressive," he said, nodding his chin at the wall. "Did you draw this?"

"Yeah." She couldn't remember a time when she didn't have crayon, paint or charcoal pencil in hand. Some art classes in high school and junior college had improved her technique and she soaked up his praise like rain on tinder-dry brush. "Thanks."

He looked down at her, his gaze assessing. "How've you been?"

"Good. You?" It hadn't been that long since she'd seen him. "Weren't you back last month right around the Fourth of July?"

"Yeah." He glanced down and shifted his feet. "Now I'm taking a working vacation."

"Oh."

In college he'd created a line of silk-screened T-shirts, jackets and hats with a Montana theme. A venture capitalist staying at the Thunder Canyon Resort had seen the items displayed in a restaurant on the premises and approached him about backing a bigger business enterprise. Marlon then expanded into MC/TC, primarily a jeans label. When the Hollywood "it" girl he was dating was photographed wearing the brand and turned up in multiple national magazines, the company took off and became phenomenally successful. And still was. But Haley didn't know anyone who wasn't feeling the effects of the recession, and wondered about the state of his company.

This teen program, ROOTS, was dependent on donations and people were struggling, just one of the reasons the opening was later than she'd hoped. But there was still about a month until school started and she wanted the kids to be able to take advantage while they could.

"How's business?" she asked.

"So-so."

She waited for more information, but he was looking around. The room was small and square. And obviously empty.

"I know it doesn't look like much now," she defended, "but I have plans. With used furniture from the Second Chances thrift store the interior will really pop." She pointed to a doorway. "There's a bathroom and tiny storage area through there, with a door leading to the parking lot. It's big enough to put in a refrigerator, microwave and cabinet for snacks and paper goods. If my brother is anything to go by, teenage boys have bottomless appetites."

"How's Angie?"

"Good," she said. "Trying to figure out what she wants to be when she grows up. She's taking classes at the junior college and changes her major every other month."

"And Austin?"

"He just graduated from college. Engineering major," she said, her voice full of the pride she couldn't hide. "There was a time when I didn't think he would graduate from high school, let alone go to college and get a degree."

"Why is that?"

"He never had a father figure and was only sixteen when mom died. That's a tough age under the best of circumstances, but the two of them were especially close. It hit him really hard."

Her brother wasn't the only one. It had been the worst time of her life and she suspected her sister Angie felt the same way.

"Yeah. I can see where that would happen."

"I'm convinced it's our roots here in Thunder Canyon that tipped the scales in his favor."

"How's that?" he asked.

"The people in this community took us under their wing. Neighbors helped out, especially Ben Walters."

"Isn't he the rancher who lives near your place?"

"Yeah. He's a widower." She sighed. "That's probably why he spent a lot of time with Austin, called him on his crap when necessary because Austin refused to pay attention to me. I'm only his big sister. Sometimes Ben just listened when the kid needed a man to talk to."

"Ben always was a saint."

The critical tone made her feel defensive for some reason. "He was a father to my brother and I'll never forget it. In fact, that's really how ROOTS started in the first place."

"Oh?"

She nodded. "They hired me at The Hitching Post when I needed a job to support the family. Folks stepped in to watch Angie while I was working. And Ben kept Austin out of trouble. We were teens without a mom and Thunder Canyon put their arms around us. I wanted to open a community clubhouse where teenagers can come. Hang out. Talk if they want. Or not. It's just a place where you don't have to feel alone. Like the way people here in town made me feel."

"ROOTS?"

"The name is from an embroidered sampler of my mother's that we keep on the wall at home. It says 'There are but two lasting things we give our children—Roots and Wings.' I intend to pay that message forward."

"Good for you."

Her eyes narrowed on him. Was he laughing at her? "I wouldn't expect a big shot entrepreneur like yourself to understand something that isn't about making money. Especially when it fell into your lap—"

He reached out and put his index finger to her lips, to silence her. "Success didn't just happen. I worked damn hard for it and still do. That wasn't a criticism. Obviously you've got one nerve left and apparently I stepped on it."

"Sorry." That happened when your buttons got pushed, and not any of the good buttons. "It's been sort of an uphill battle—finding the money, convincing the mayor and town council of the need... Thunder Canyon High's principal and faculty have been incredibly helpful. And my special adviser is Carleigh Benedict, from county social services." She

took a deep breath. "There will be strict cur-
fews enforced. And adult supervision when
the doors are open. I want to make sure I get
everything right."

He looked down for a moment, then met
her gaze. "Sounds like an ambitious undertaking. Could you use an extra pair of
hands?"

Surely he wasn't talking about himself.
"I'm definitely going to need volunteers.
When it becomes the coolest hangout in town,
which is what I'm hoping for. But right now
it's just me."

"That wasn't me gathering information. It
was a sincere offer to be of assistance," he
explained, his expression wry.

"You want to help out?" she asked skeptically.

"Don't sound so surprised." His eyes
turned a darker shade of brown, but hurting Marlon's feelings seemed like a long shot
since there'd never been an abundance of evidence that he had any. "Like I said, my sched-
ule is loose and not being busy makes me
nuts. It seems like a win-win."

"You could give your dad a hand," she suggested helpfully. His father, Frank, owned
Cates Construction where Marlon's identi-

cal twin, Matt, worked, the twin expected to take over the business some day. She marveled at how different the two men with the same face were. Matt was serious and a stay-put kind of guy. Marlon was a charmer who never stood still.

"I plan to help out my dad if he needs it," he said. "But you know as well as I do that things have slowed down in construction and he's doing his best not to lay off workers. Especially the ones with families."

"Times are tough. That's going to affect a lot of kids," she agreed.

"So let me help you out."

On top of more surprise that he wouldn't drop the idea, Haley's suspicions kicked in. His reputation had bad boy written all over it. Whoever supervised at ROOTS would have to be someone the kids looked up to. Not that she thought Marlon was a threat, but he wasn't positive role model material either.

"I don't think there's much to do right now," she lied.

"Could have fooled me." One of his dark eyebrows rose as he looked around at the empty space and three remaining dingy green walls. "Look, Haley, you'd be doing me a favor and I could return it."

She bit her lip as she looked up at him, trying to figure out how to say this in the nicest possible way. "The thing is, Marlon, what I'm trying to do here is important. These are kids who have been let down in one way or another. Like you said, people are losing their jobs and the bad stuff filters down to the kids. In a world where nothing is in their control they need someone they can count on."

"And you don't think I'm reliable?"

From personal experience she knew he wasn't. A long time ago he'd kissed her and promised to call. He never did. She'd waited by the phone, slept with it next to the bed, constantly checked for messages. There was no way she would have missed his call, if there'd been one. On top of that, he breezed in and out of town whenever he felt like it. He couldn't be counted on.

When she didn't answer immediately, he said, "What's your point?" His facial expression didn't change, but there was an edge to his voice.

Darn it, she thought. He was going to make her say it straight out. She looked up at him, way up, and took a deep breath. "I just don't think commitment is one of your strengths,

Marlon. But I really appreciate the offer. Thanks anyway."

He nodded once, then left without another word, which made her one part sad and two parts grateful. Her crush was part of her past, but it didn't seem wise to test that theory by having him underfoot. Although when she looked around and thought about her to-do list, she had a sinking feeling she'd just cut off her nose to spite her face.

"Just once," she whispered to the grungy walls, "I'd like to get what I wish for."

She wished Marlon hadn't walked in. And that he wasn't still the handsome scoundrel she remembered. Most of all she wished to be someone he might be interested in. But she knew better than most that life was filled with challenges you had no control over and some you did. And Marlon Cates was one she just wasn't willing to take on.

Commitment wasn't his strength?

After several hours of stewing over those words, Marlon Cates pushed aside the see-through lace curtain as he stared down on Main Street from the window of his apartment over The Hitching Post. He'd rented the western-themed place, with brass bed, antique chifforobe and its own bath, for a month. It was within walking distance of ROOTS where he'd intended to do his court-mandated time to get back his driving privileges. His parents and three brothers knew what had happened and his mother didn't sugarcoat anything when she said it served him right. Three speeding tickets in less than a year landed him in front of a judge who yanked his license and gave him thirty days of community service.

From this vantage point he could see the storefront where he planned to do his time. When the court clerk gave him a list of places, he'd spotted Haley Anderson's name and decided it might not be so bad after all.

But she'd told him very politely, thank you, no. She was definitely not like the girl he'd kissed all those years ago. He remembered the sweet little sound she'd made when their lips touched, but not how pretty she was. He also didn't remember this confidence, with just enough contrariness to make her interesting. And really artistic judging by the mural she was creating.

He could have told her why he'd offered to help. He'd actually planned to because she would have to know eventually. There would be legal paperwork from the court that she had to sign off on. The thing was she'd gone on about why she was starting the program. Raising her younger siblings after her mom's death. Being part of the community. Bending over backward to get the teen meeting spot right.

Her earnestness was daunting. It seemed pure, but he'd had a costly lesson in misjudging women. A mistake he wouldn't repeat. Still, he just couldn't bring himself to tell her the whole truth of his offer to help. Since he wasn't getting out of Thunder Canyon without a driver's license, he had to persuade Haley to give him a chance. He'd prove himself trustworthy and indispensable, then break the news about community service. It was a good plan and there was no reason to doubt that he'd achieve his objective.

Sales were his business and women found him charming. Mostly. Because there were so few exceptions, they were memorable. There was the girl in college who could give lessons in sales. She'd made him fall for her and even propose. She'd insisted wedding should come before bedding but she wouldn't feel right about marrying him until she paid off a large debt—medical bills from her father's open heart surgery.

Marlon knew now he hadn't been thinking with his head when he wrote her name on a check with a lot of zeroes and handed it over. It was the last time he saw her.

His most recent charm-resistant woman was the judge who'd revoked his license for thirty days. Her Honor just didn't understand the need for speed on the empty, open highway and how it cleared a guy's head. And he was a guy with a lot on his mind.

He'd found his community service. Unfortunately it was for another woman who didn't seem to get his charm. He could go to the next organization on the court's list, but Haley Anderson's turndown had tapped into his mother lode of stubborn. He was going to change her mind. And the prospect was more entertaining than he would have expected.

Marlon saw Haley's old, beat-up blue Ford truck go slowly by The Hitching Post, pull around the corner and into the parking lot behind ROOTS. There was a refrigerator in the truck bed and he got an idea that might solve his problem.

He grinned. It was time to amp up the charm.

He left his apartment and walked down the wooden stairs, leaving by the back entrance to avoid going through the bar and grill. The breakfast and lunch rushes were over and the place sounded pretty empty, but it was too easy to get pulled into a conversation. He was a man on a mission.

He rounded the building, then walked down Main Street, turned right on Nugget Way and into the parking lot behind ROOTS. Haley was standing in front of the half-glass, half-wood door, unlocking it.

"Hi," he said.

She whirled around at the sound of his voice and pressed a hand to her chest. "You scared me."

"Sorry." The sound of his boots on the paved parking lot was loud enough to wake the dead. She must have a lot on her mind, too. "I thought you heard me."

She shook her head, then tucked a strand of hair that escaped her ponytail behind her ear. Earlier when she was painting, her hair had been twisted up and held with a comb thing. An image of that shiny brown silk loose around her shoulders flashed through his mind as the need to run his fingers through it banged around in his gut. He folded his arms over his chest to rein himself in. Distractions were not permitted to men on missions.

She'd changed out of the earlier ratty jeans and oversize T-shirt into a red tab-front, collared shirt with a yellow horse and bridle above the words The Hitching Post on the breast. The shirt was tucked into the waistband of a pair of denims that hugged her curvy hips and thighs. Her big brown eyes assessed him warily. The expression reminded him of a potential client at a sales meeting, wondering what he wanted them to buy and how much it was going to cost.

From experience he knew it was best not to lead with his bottom line. Get your target's guard down.

"Nice day," he said, glancing up at a blue sky with wispy white clouds floating lazily by.

Haley looked up, then back at him. "Yes, it is. A little warm, though," she added.

"Really? You think so?" Maybe he was making her warm, which wouldn't be a bad thing. Unless it increased her caution quotient. One look at her lips pressed tightly together told him that was the case. He let his gaze wander to the towering peaks in the distance.

"The mountains here are different from the ones in L.A."

He had a condo near the beach in Marina del Rey, a short drive from where his company MC/TC was headquartered. The high energy of the bustling business center couldn't be more different from Thunder Canyon, Montana.

"How are they different?" Haley asked. "Other than the fact that here you can actually see them."

"Ah, a subtle Los Angeles smog dig?"

"Was that subtle? I didn't mean to be."

"For your information, the California emission standards are actually making a difference in air quality."

"Good to know. But I prefer not to see the air I'm sucking in. I hope Thunder Canyon never has to clean up what we breathe because of too many cars on the road."

Now he was feeling the heat. Cars were not a subject he wanted highlighted in this conversation, since for the next month it would be illegal for him to drive one. Not only that, her eyes were still wondering what he was after.

He glanced at her truck, standing beside them. "I couldn't help noticing you have a refrigerator in your vehicle."

Her full lips curved up for a moment, chasing the guarded look from her eyes. "Nothing gets by you, does it?"

He laughed. "Just a little something you picked up?"

"It's a donation to the teen center," she explained.

"How are you going to get it inside?"

"That's a very good question." She looked from the big white appliance to the back door of the center. "I figured I'd grab some burly men at The Hitching Post and impose on their good nature."

"I'm burly and here now. And my good nature is legendary. Impose away."

She folded her arms over her chest. "You're going to move that heavy white albatross and put it where I say?"

"That's the plan."

"Don't tell me," she said. "There's a big letter S on your chest. The superhero swoops in to save the day."

He eyed the appliance critically and shook his head. "I was thinking more of two planks, a dolly and some strategically placed straps, then rolling it inside all by my lonesome."

"And just where would you get all that paraphernalia?" she asked suspiciously. "Wait, in your back pocket."

He shook his finger at her, a teasing reprimand. "You're going to be sorry for mocking me."

"It's worth the risk." The distrustful look slid back into her eyes.

The expression on her face spoke volumes about the fact that she didn't expect him to follow through. Based on their brief contact six years ago, he supposed it was understandable. But this was now, they were adults, and he had something to prove.

"Just remember," he said. "An apology is always good form when one is confirmed to be in the wrong."

Marlon reached for his cell phone and made a quick call to the Cates Construction office. "Give me thirty minutes and I'll have that big boy inside ROOTS for you."

"Right," she said skeptically.

While he waited for his twin brother to bring what he needed, he helped Haley unload the paper goods from the cab of her truck. There were bags of plates, napkins, cups. They carried them into the small storage area off the main room.

When they came out again, there was a

truck parked behind hers with the words Cates Construction painted on the side. His twin brother, Matt, hopped out.

"Hi, Haley," he said.

"Matt. I guess you're here to bail out your brother and make good on his promise?"

"Nope. I just brought the stuff he asked for. He's on his own. I've got work to do."

Marlon helped Matt unload everything, thanked him, and watched him drive back to the construction site for Connor McFarlane's new house.

Haley was staring after the truck, then met his gaze. "When you look at your brother is it like staring into a mirror?"

He laughed and shook his head. "We're pretty different. My mother doesn't have any trouble telling us apart. Although she did admit to being challenged when one of us calls her on the phone."

"Double trouble," Haley murmured. "Okay, hotshot, let's see if your burly body can cash the check your big mouth wrote."

"Oh, ye of little faith."

He let down her truck's tailgate and settled the two sturdy planks side by side about the width of the dolly's wheels. Then he put it in the bed, hauled himself up and muscled the refrigerator onto it. He strapped it on, tilted it back, and wheeled it easily down before rolling it toward the open door.

"Where did you want this?" he asked.

"In the storage room. There's an outlet in there to plug it in," she explained.

He moved it inside and followed her instructions. The sound of the fridge humming made him grin when he met her gaze. "Anything else?"

Her sheepish expression was satisfying. "Thank you very much."

"You're welcome." He arched one eyebrow. "Is there anything more you'd like to say?"

"It's not very gentlemanly to make a woman grovel."

"Hmm." He leaned an arm on the dolly's curved handle. "I believe I warned you about mocking me."

She rubbed a finger across the side of her nose. "Okay. I'll say it. I was wrong, Marlon. I appreciate your help."

"What would you do without me?"

"Same as I do when you're not here," she answered. "Wing it."

"The thing is, Haley, I'm here now. Let me help you out."

"That's okay. I'm used to handling things on my own."

Marlon wasn't used to women turning him down and that was twice she'd told him no. It was really starting to tick him off. The next time he asked she would say yes.

She just didn't know it yet.

Chapter Two

Haley waited for Marlon to take the hint and leave, despite feeling kind of bad about it. He really had saved her a whole lot of time and a great deal of trouble.

"Look, Haley—" His easygoing manner didn't change, but something slid into his dark eyes that looked a lot like determination. "With my help, you can accomplish twice as much in half the time."

There was no way to refute that. She was racing against the clock, even if it was her own self-imposed deadline. But the Marlon she remembered wasn't all that enthusiastic about helping others. And the Marlon standing in this tiny storage room seemed to fill up the small space.

She could smell the pleasantly masculine fragrance of his skin and feel the heat from his body. Either was enough to short-circuit rational thought, but the combination made her lightheaded and jumpy. She walked out into the big, empty room with its half-finished mural.

"Two heads are better than one," he continued, following her.

"And that would be helpful—how?"

He rested his hands on lean hips and looked around. "I assume you're going to put something in here."

"Furniture," she confirmed.

"I could help."

"Uh-huh." If he was around—and that was a very big if.

"And I can provide a guy's point of view."

"For?" she asked.

"When the kids come around. If they're having a problem, I can give you the male slant on it." There was a serious expression on his face, but the twinkle in his eyes gave him away. "This might come as a big surprise to you, but men and women don't think the same way."

She found herself fighting a smile. "Actually, I think I knew that."

At least she'd probably read something about it in a magazine or seen evidence in a movie. Real life, not so much. She hadn't dated in high school, and the short time she'd spent in college didn't give her the chance to really know the guy she'd been seeing. Then her mom died and she'd come home. A personal life was so far down her priority list it never happened.

"Okay, so you can see the benefit I could provide."

"It's the content of that benefit that concerns me," she said.

"How so?"

"The kids need a role model." She stopped there and hoped he would fill in the blanks.

He stared at her for several moments. "From that I take it you don't think I would be a positive influence?"

Bingo. "Word on the street is that you're a rule-breaker and envelope-pusher."

"Some would say I think outside the box. That's not necessarily a bad quality."

"The thing about breaking rules," she said, "is that you have to know what they are before pushing them. The kids are in that vulnerable limbo where they're figuring things out."

"I can help with that."

Like he'd helped her six years ago? That's not the kind of lesson she wanted the teens to get from ROOTS.

"How?" she asked skeptically.

"You always did the right thing and can't understand the thought process of walking on the wild side. I can give you a different slant."

"Is that an admission of guilt?" she asked, surprised.

"It's a confession insofar as I admit to getting away with 'stuff'. My point being that not much gets by me. But you don't have the same experiences that give one a certain skill set. We would come at any problem of the kids' from two different viewpoints."

"I appreciate the offer, Marlon—"

"Don't say it," he warned.

"What?"

"You were going to say you appreciate the offer, but I shouldn't hold my breath."

"I guess you're a mind reader." Not.

If so he'd know how real rejection felt. For days after he'd promised to call it felt as if she'd held her breath. When she finally realized he didn't plan to contact her, it had hurt a lot. But she figured a man like Marlon didn't know what it was like to be let down.

His eyes narrowed. "You know, Haley, this is beginning to feel personal."

"Excuse me?" Her heart started to beat a little faster and the question might buy her some time to slow it down. "I think of it as practical, actually."

"And I disagree." He ran his fingers through his hair. "Practical would be taking what's offered because you need the help. Since you're turning me down, it's got to be personal."

"How do you know I don't have a long waiting list of offers?" she bluffed.

"For starters, you'd have lined someone up to help you get that refrigerator inside. But you planned to wing it."

So she wasn't a very good bluffer. He was way too close to the truth with that personal remark. Who'd have guessed that Marlon Cates was so perceptive? There was no way she would give him the satisfaction of knowing that his rejection still tweaked her on any level, no matter how small.

"It's not personal," she assured him. "I just have to do what's best for the center."

"So we're back to me being unreliable."

"Everyone knows you have a multi-million-dollar company to run," she hedged. "It's just common sense that you can't be counted on when you have to focus on your business."

"Shouldn't I be the one who gets to decide how much time I have to spare for a worthy cause?" He stared at her intently. "And aren't you, as the driving force behind this venture, the one who takes whatever anyone is willing to donate?"

He had a point, darn it. If he hadn't started his multi-million-dollar company, he could easily have gone into the practice of law. He'd certainly backed her into a corner that was going to take some slick maneuvering to get out of gracefully. What she wanted to say was, what happens when you leave again? Because he was leaving. His life wasn't in Thunder Canyon anymore.

"Look," he said when she was quiet. "How about this. I'll commit to a certain number of hours per week for the next four weeks. If I prove to be unreliable, I'll do the right thing and admit I was wrong."

She sighed. "Okay."

He opened his mouth, then shut it again and stared for several moments. "What?"

"I agree to your proposal." She met his

gaze. "But it's only fair to warn you that you're on probation. My probation. If you mess up even once, you're gone. I can't take the chance with the kids."

He held out his hand. "Done."

She stared for several moments and her gaze slid up his strong arm. Finally she settled her fingers into his palm and shook on the deal.

"You won't be sorry."

When the words were followed by a signature Marlon Cates grin, Haley was already sorry. The fluttering in her stomach and the tightness in her chest made her sorry. He still affected her. His presence made her feel things it wasn't safe to feel.

But really, it was one month. Thirty days. Not enough time to do any damage because she was wise to him. She knew to not expect anything.

Only a fool with stars in her eyes would let her guard down and Haley Anderson hadn't had stars in her eyes for a very long time.

Several hours later Haley was willing to admit, if only to herself, that Marlon's help had come in handy. And his timing for offering it couldn't have been better. Second

Chances had agreed to donate furniture to her cause.

With Marlon's help, she'd moved over an eight-foot sofa with worn seat cushions and a threadbare loveseat that didn't match. There was a faux leather recliner that didn't recline, coffee and end tables with cigarette burns and scratches. Carved into the top of one were the initials CS+WR, with a heart surrounding the whole thing. Very romantic. The big, ugly donated lamps covered some of the dings, but she arranged it so the heart still showed.

They also got a TV. Since broadcast television had switched from analog to digital, quite a few sets had been discarded. Haley was more than happy to let the thrift store donate one to ROOTS because she had a converter box. Now it was all set up on a stand in the corner.

She brushed her forearm across her forehead and grinned. "Awesome."

"You think?"

Haley heard the doubt in his voice. "Beauty is in the eye of the beholder."

Marlon stood beside her and folded his arms over his chest as he surveyed the room, his gaze settling on the place where stuffing was coming out of the gold-and-brown striped sofa cushion. Then he looked at the green-and-pink loveseat sitting at a right angle to it. "You call this beautiful and can actually say that with a straight face?"

"I still have a little money left from donations to buy some ready-made slipcovers that will just make this room pop." She looked up at him and could almost hear her heart making a popping sound.

It was best to ignore that and concentrate on the good stuff—like being way ahead of where she'd expected to be right now. The only plan she'd had was for her brother and sister to get off work at Thunder Canyon Resort and stop by to help. But there was a flaw in Plan A, which Angie and Austin had pointed out in tones that bordered on whiney. After work they'd be hungry and tired and not in favor of moving furniture. They'd reluctantly agreed to help, but now it wasn't necessary.

Because she'd had Marlon.

No, he wasn't hers. She didn't have him. She had the time he'd donated. No more, no less. And she still couldn't figure out why he'd insisted on helping. One of these days she'd stop looking a gift horse in the mouth while waiting for the other shoe to fall.

"I say it looks good," she said, nodding firmly.

His expression said he disagreed. "That depends on your definition of good and your standards."

"That's the beauty. It's not my standards that matter. This is for the kids. It's going to get trashed, anyway. They don't need to worry about ruining something that's brand-new. This room says come on in. Be comfortable."

"And you couldn't have done it without me," he teased.

"I could have," she said, then reluctantly added, "but not this fast. Seriously, Marlon, thank you."

"You're welcome."

The deep, slightly husky quality in his voice scraped over her skin and seeped inside, tying her in knots. On top of that she was tongue-tied, too. He was a glib, quick-witted, millionaire man of the world and she was a nobody from a small town in Montana. It shouldn't matter, but it did. And as silence stretched between them, she felt more and more awkward and unsophisticated.

Just before she wished the earth would open and swallow her whole, the door opened and her brother and sister walked in. Relief flooded through her. "Austin. Angie."

Her brother was as tall as Marlon and at twenty-two he wasn't that much younger. His brown hair was cut short and with a lot of time and product, he got it to stick out in the trendiest possible way. His navy blue T-shirt set off the dark brown eyes that were studying the man beside her.

"Hey, Marlon." He stuck out his hand.

For some reason the gesture seemed especially manly of her brother and made Haley proud.

"Austin." He shook her brother's hand. "How are you?"

"Good. You?"

"Can't complain." He nodded to Angie. "You look more like your big sister every time I see you."

The slender, twenty-year-old's cheeks turned as pink as her T-shirt. She tucked a strand of straight, shiny, shoulder-length brown hair behind her ear. "Is that a compliment?"

He glanced down at Haley and winked. "Of course."

Like she believed that. What was he going to say? The Anderson sisters shouldn't go down Main Street Thunder Canyon without bags over their heads? Charm and blarney were his specialties.

Austin's gaze drifted past them to the furniture in the center of the room, arranged in a cozy square to cultivate conversation. "So, we're too late to help?" he asked, grinning.

"Try not to look so disappointed," Haley said, wryly.

"Darn, I was really looking forward to lugging stuff around." If anything, his smile grew wider.

"Marlon was kind enough to help me."

Austin nodded. "I owe you one, man."

"No one's counting. I'm happy to be of service." The man looked down at her. "And believe me, it wasn't easy."

That goes double for me, Haley thought, meeting his gaze. "The point is that the basics are in place and I'll get the word out that the kids can come on in."

Angie nodded at the half-finished mural. "It looks good, Haley. I like what you did with the cell phones, computers and books. The sports stuff is cool, too. Very yin and yang."

"Balance. It's a subtle message up there, but it's the goal." Haley glanced over her shoulder and smiled at her work in progress.

"And a good one," her brother said. "But I really am glad Marlon gave you a hand. It's been a long day."

"Austin works in engineering at the resort," Haley explained.

"Maintenance actually," he clarified. "Angie's in housekeeping."

Her sister shrugged. "It's a job."

"You should be grateful to have it," Haley pointed out.

"So you keep telling me." Her sister's lips pulled tight.

"Hey, sis," Austin said, nudging his younger sister's arm with his elbow and effectively filling the tense silence. "Now that we don't have to help, we can eat sooner. Remember we're starving."

"Yeah."

Haley nodded. "Okay. I've done all I can here for tonight. You guys head on home and I'll be along to get dinner started."

"I can make dinner," Angie offered.

"That's okay." Austin's expression kaleidoscoped from horror to sympathetic understanding. "The last time you got near the stove and tried anything but a sandwich or cold cereal, the scream of the smoke detector took out my hearing for hours."

"It was a blessing in disguise," Haley said. "Always good to know they work."

But when Angie's brown eyes darkened with temper, it was clear she didn't appreciate the good-natured joking. "And you've never let me try again. How am I going to learn?"

"Have you ever heard the expression where there's smoke, there's fire?" Austin's mouth curved up in a teasing smile. "I kind of like having a roof over my head. Especially with winter coming."

"You're a jerk." Angie punched him in the arm.

"Ow." He rubbed the spot and said to Haley, "She hit me. Are you going to let her get away with not using her words?"

"When are you going to stop treating me like a kid? I'm older than you were when mom died." Angie glared at her, then turned on her heel and walked out, slamming the door behind her.

"She's a little touchy." Austin shrugged. "I better go after her. I'm her ride."

"See you at home," Haley said.

When they were alone again, she and Marlon both spoke at once.

"I'm sorry—"

"They grew up—"

Haley shrugged. "You go first."

"I was just going to say that your siblings grew up well, thanks to you."

She stared out the window where dusk was just settling over Main Street. "I was just going to say that I'm sorry you had to see that."

"What?" he asked innocently.

"Angie's meltdown. She gets snippy when she thinks I'm babying her."

"Looks to me like you were just taking care of your own." He shrugged.

"She doesn't see it that way. She thinks twenty years old is all grown up."

His brown eyes turned the color of rich chocolate when sympathy slid into them. "She's right, though. She is older than you were when—" he shifted his feet then looked at her "—when you took over as head of the family."

"I did what I had to. What anyone would have."

"I'm not so sure that's true. A lot of people would have just walked away from all that responsibility. Not you."

"I couldn't. They're my family." She shrugged as if that explained everything.

"And family is there for each other. But that's not how it looked to me. From what I saw, you take care of everyone else. I can't help wondering who takes care of you."

"Like I said, I don't need anyone. I'm just fine on my own."

He shook his head as he stared down at her. "I'm two parts awed and one part bothered by that."

"Why?"

"As the song says, everybody needs somebody sometime. Like you needed me today."

"That's the thing, Marlon. If you hadn't been here, I'd have rounded up some guys. Austin would have helped. He has friends. I'd have gotten it done somehow."

She remembered back to those first weeks and months after her mother died. They'd gone through the motions of living, but it was like being among the walking dead. They were in shock. In spite of that, she'd had to make sure her siblings went to school, ate, did their homework. That evolved into supervising who their friends were, where they went and with whom. All the things a parent would do. What her mom had done for her.

"You're pretty amazing, Haley Anderson."

"Thanks."

His praise warmed her clear through, in a place that she hadn't realized was frozen over and numb. But it was dangerous to allow it to thaw. If that happened, feeling would return and with it the pins and needles of nerve endings awakening and the pain that went along with it. She'd gotten through her mom's death, but never ever wanted to lose someone again. She just didn't think she had it in her to go on without someone she loved.

And Marlon Cates, happy wanderer and world traveler, was not the person she wanted to talk to about this. It was like exposing her soft underbelly and left her feeling too vulnerable, too raw.

She angled her head toward the door. "I have to go. The hungry hordes are waiting at home."

"Right," he said. "Me, too."

"Okay." She grabbed her purse from the floor and slid the strap over her shoulder. "Good night."

"Wait." He put his hand on her arm to stop her. The feel of his fingers rolled heat all the way to her heart, which started popping like a bag of microwave popcorn. Just barely, she stopped the quiver that his touch generated.

"What?" she asked, a little too breathlessly. With luck he didn't notice.

"What time do you want me here tomorrow?"

Putting a finer point on the question, she didn't really want him there at all. Because she would look forward to seeing him. And she didn't want to.

But apparently whatever selfless kick he was on hadn't let up because he was waiting for an answer. "I'm working the breakfast and dinner shifts at The Hitching Post, but this mural needs work so I plan to do that for a couple of hours in between. You could scrub the walls." His narrowed gaze made her add, "I can't afford more paint, but it needs to be cleaned up. Just a little elbow grease." A task that just might flip the off switch on this altruistic streak of his.

"Okay. See you then."

When he took his hand off her arm and walked out the door, Haley released the breath she'd been holding. Anticipation stretched inside her, a sensation she hadn't experienced for a long time. If she could have stopped it she would have because it so wasn't a good idea. But the fact was, she found herself looking forward to tomorrow—and dreading it.

What else would he talk her into doing against her better judgment?

Chapter Three

When Haley arrived at ROOTS the next day Marlon was there waiting. She pulled up at the curb, then grabbed the bags of stuff sitting on the seat beside her and hopped down.

"Hi."

Just like that, his voice and smile kickstarted that popping inside her, even though she'd had a whole lot of hours to brace for another face-to-face. "Hi."

Clever comeback, she told herself.

"Let me take those," he said, reaching for the bags.

Their hands brushed and her chest felt tight. "Thanks."

He hefted one. "Do you have rocks in here?"

"You caught me." Slightly more clever on the comeback scale.

He peeked inside and saw the bottles of cleaning supplies along with a bag of candy. There was a wry expression in his eyes. "Nutritious."

"Special treats," she defended. "There's a couple cases of soda in the truck. I'll get them."

He set the bags down by the door and said, "Allow me. You be the brains. I'll be the brawn."

Don't have to ask me twice, she thought, letting herself look at his back as he walked to her truck. She was twenty-four-years old and had never had sex, but inexperience didn't stop her from admiring his broad shoulders and excellent butt. She didn't even know the criteria upon which veteran, male-watching women relied to determine whether or not a man had a bonafide excellent backside, but to her way of thinking, Marlon definitely did.

The muscles in his arms and back rippled and bunched as he stacked the cases of soda one on top of the other then lifted. A flutter moved from her belly to her throat and all of a sudden she couldn't draw a deep breath.

As he turned, she quickly stuck her key in the door and hoped he hadn't caught her staring. That was all she needed. Having him around was a challenge, but she wouldn't know how to handle his teasing about man/woman stuff, highlighting her lack of sophistication. She just wouldn't be able to stand it if he pitied her.

He stopped beside her and frowned. "Is there a problem with the door?"

"Lock's a little stiff," she mumbled, turning the key and twisting the knob to open the door for him.

He walked in ahead of her and she picked up one of the bags outside before following him. Inside, she saw that he'd stopped dead-still and everything about his body language screamed tension.

"Haley?"

"What?" She moved around him and glanced at the room.

It wasn't the way she'd left it. The back cushions on the sofa had been moved. There were junk food wrappers and beer cans on the coffee table.

"Did you have chips and beer for dinner here last night?"

"No." The one word came out on a whisper as apprehension ballooned inside her.

"Did you let some kids in?" he asked.

"I left right after you. ROOTS isn't officially opened yet. And if it were, I wouldn't be serving beer."

Marlon set the cases of soda down on the scarred coffee table. "Stay here."

"Why? Where are you going?" She automatically started toward the back and he put out his arm to stop her.

"What part of 'stay here' did you not understand?"

"The part where you're going all special agent, covert op. This is my project."

"And there could be someone back there who knows it and is waiting for you." He glared down and there was no trace of humor in his eyes, which was more alarming than the tension in his voice. "Stand by the open door. I'm going to check the place out. If necessary, you go for help."

"But, Marlon, you might need me—"

"No," he said firmly. "Stay here."

"Okay."

It took less than a minute for him to look around the storeroom and bathroom, but it felt like days. Bad stuff always seemed to last longer than the good.

"It's all clear." He appeared in the doorway, his face grim. "But you've got a broken window in here."

She hurried back and saw that the glass in the top half of the door had been shattered. Shards were on the floor. "That's how they got in."

"Yeah."

"Why can't I catch a break?"

The words popped out before she could stop them. She'd been so excited when she left last night. The kids would have a place to sit and TV to watch. Now someone who only wanted a place to party had violated her sense of trust.

"Sometimes life is just not fair—" Emotion flooded her and she caught the corner of her top lip between her teeth to keep from giving in to it.

Marlon pulled her into his arms. "Don't go to the bad place."

"I don't have to go. It broke in and made itself at home."

His big palm rubbed up and down her back and the heat of his body warmed hers. She hadn't even realized how cold she was.

"Don't let it get to you. We'll talk to the cops and see if there's anything they can do. Look on the bright side."

"Is there one?" She forced herself to step away from him. "No, wait, this is where you say things could have been worse."

"It's true."

"Yeah? How?"

"There wasn't anything here to take. And they brought their own beer and snacks," he added.

She fought a smile and felt better for it. God help her, she was glad he'd been here. She wasn't used to anyone looking out for her. Leaning on him was different. And not totally bad. This was a side to Marlon that she'd never seen before. Kind of heroic, which was out of character. She remembered him being a scoundrel and everything she'd seen and heard had supported that impression.

"Let's not wallow," he suggested.

"Not even for a couple minutes?"

He shook his head. "Action is what you need. I'll sweep up the glass. Do you have a measuring tape?" When she nodded, he said, "You measure for a new window. Then we'll go to the hardware store. It'll be good as new."

It was impossible not to perk up the way he was snapping out orders. She wondered what he was like to work for.

Haley handed him the broom. "So, do your employees cower in fear when they see you coming?"

"No. I'm the world's best boss."

"How do you figure?"

"I'm not in the office all that much."

"Where do you go?" she asked.

"The better question is where don't I go." He pulled the trash can over, then squatted down and picked up the biggest pieces of glass.

"Okay. I'll bite. Where don't you go?" she asked.

"Fiji. Polynesia. Tahiti." He looked up and grinned.

"Seriously."

"I've been all over the U.S. San Francisco. Seattle. New York. Washington, D.C."

"Why?"

"I'm a salesman. It's my job to meet with business people and convince them that the MC/TC brand will fly out of their stores."

"I bet you could probably sell beachfront property in Las Vegas," she said.

"It wouldn't be easy." He looked up and grinned. "But challenge is my middle name."

"Have you been to Las Vegas?"

"Quite a few times. They say New York is the city that never sleeps, but Vegas is the real deal. Very exciting. A buffet for the senses."

"How so?"

He stood and leaned on the broom. "The first thing you notice are the lights. The Strip is all neon and turns night into day. Then you go inside and there are more lights, this time with the sound. Dings, bells, sirens. Any kind of food you can imagine is there. In fact, any decadence you're looking for you can find."

"Wow." She couldn't help wondering how many decadences he'd had. "Where else have you been?"

"The beach. Caribbean beaches are spectacular, but Malibu, Santa Barbara, Santa Monica—there's an excitement to the California coast."

"I've never seen the ocean," she admitted.

He met her gaze and his expression was perilously close to pity. "No?"

She shook her head, then busied herself pulling out the jagged glass remaining in the top of the door. "I've never been out of Montana."

"Be careful. Don't cut yourself," he warned.

"Don't worry about me."

"Easier said than done," he muttered, then asked, "Wouldn't you like to travel?"

"I don't think I'd find anything as beautiful as I've got here."

"I'm not saying Thunder Canyon isn't spectacular. But it's exciting to see other places."

"I guess I'll have to take your word on that," she said measuring the empty space where the window used to be.

She didn't cut herself on the glass, but that didn't mean she wasn't dinged. For those few moments when he'd held her in his arms she'd been able to forget that he didn't hang his hat in Thunder Canyon. But now his words brought her down to earth. It was a reminder that he might have family in town, but this wasn't where he made his home.

However generous he might be with his time right now, he'd be leaving and she shouldn't get used to having him around permanently.

But those few moments in his arms had been nicer than she would ever have imagined, much sweeter than she wanted them to be.

* * *

"Look, you don't have to stay here with me, Marlon. It's nearly midnight."

And Marlon had been alone with Haley since it got dark. He knew he was going to have to tell her pretty soon why he was volunteering at ROOTS, but now wasn't the time. Another night had passed, another break-in had occurred and she was determined to get to the bottom of it. She had a lot on her mind and he was more than happy to use the excuse that it was wrong to add to her burdens. Mostly he was dreading the look of betrayal in her eyes when she found out. Call him a coward, but it could be put off just a little longer.

"No way I'm leaving," he said.

"Seriously, go home and get some sleep."

"Right," he said wryly. "Like I could sleep while you wait here alone for a serial killer."

"He hasn't killed anyone yet," she pointed out.

"That we know of," he reminded her.

Marlon was having serious doubts about his decision to stay and it had nothing to do with danger and everything to do with the scent of Haley's skin. They were sitting on the floor at ROOTS, resting against the back of the ratty old sofa, out of sight from the front window and facing the doorway to the rear entrance.

It was dark, not pitch black, but enough that he couldn't see her features clearly. But he could smell the sweet, floral fragrance of her and there was a knot of need twisting in his gut. He was having a hell of a time not kissing her. And since all his senses besides sight were heightened, he could practically hear the soft, moany, girlish noise she'd made the first, last and only time he'd kissed her.

That was six years ago and the memory picked now to torture him.

"Did you hear me, Marlon?"

It was like she could read his mind. "What?"

"I said, you really should go. If the guy comes back I'll just call 9-1-1. I've got my phone."

If only he could. Life would be less complicated. But his mother would give him hell and his father would have his hide. He might bend the speed limit rules, but he wasn't a slug who would leave a defenseless woman to face an intruder.

"I'm not going to argue with you, Haley. Two nights in a row someone got in—"

"That's because the hardware store didn't have the size glass I need. We knew the patch was iffy." She shifted on the hard floor and bumped him. "And the someone is a he."

"How can you be so sure?"

"The toilet seat was left up," she said confidently.

"So speaks the crime scene investigator. All the more reason I should stay and back you up."

Against the wall with his mouth against hers, kissing the living daylights out of her. And he told himself he wasn't completely selfish. If she had as much pent-up passion inside her as he thought, an explosion of it would chase the sadness from her eyes.

It was always there, hovering, unless she was excited about something, like this project to pay it forward. Or when she was ticked off at him. Wouldn't it be interesting to see if she was as responsive as he suspected in other ways? If kissing her wouldn't complicate the hell out of everything, he'd do it and move on because concentrating on life after community service was hard when she looked so sad.

"Okay," she said, yawning. "You can stay. But I hope he comes soon."

That went double for him. When her shoulder brushed his arm, his skin caught fire and the blood drained from his head and pumped to points south of his belt.

Haley squirmed around, trying to get comfortable. "If he doesn't want to get caught, you'd think he'd pick somewhere else to break in."

"You wanted this place to be somewhere the kids would feel welcome," he reminded her. "Obviously this guy got the vibe."

And speaking of vibes, he needed to take his mind off the ones that urged him to pull her into his arms. "So what do you think about Bo Clifton running for mayor?"

"I'm all for it. He's my best friend's cousin."

"I didn't know you and Elise Clifton were friends," he said and felt her shrug.

"She was a year older than me, but somehow we bonded. I think it had something to do with the fact that neither of us had a father."

Elise Clifton's father had been murdered when she was twelve years old. Marlon didn't know Haley's story, but he heard the sadness in her voice. Though he couldn't see her expression, he knew there would be sadness there, too. "What happened to your dad?"

"Beats me. He just left. I don't really remember him."

Marlon waited for her to say more, but she didn't. "Do you want to talk about it?"

"No."

"Okay, then." He moved off of the sensitive subject. "What chance do you think Bo has in the election, now that he's thrown his hat in the ring?"

"It's hard to say. Arthur Swinton has been around for years. He's experienced and everyone knows him. It's hard to argue against a family values platform."

It would be especially important to someone like Haley who had stepped into a difficult situation to take care of family, he thought. "What do you think of Bo?"

There was silence for a few moments before she said, "He's young and has fresh ideas that could shake things up. That's not a bad thing. Especially with the economy in such big trouble."

"You got that right."

"Has your company been affected by the downturn?" she asked.

"Oh, yeah." It was one of the things on his mind when he'd been pulled over for speeding. He'd been wondering whether to tough it out or sell out. The latter option would mean putting a lot of people out of work. That was something he didn't take lightly.

"What's wrong, Marlon?"

"Why?"

"I could hear it in your voice. Something's bothering you."

Apparently he wasn't the only one whose other senses were heightened in the dark. "I just have some business things to work through."

"Anything I can—" A noise at the back door stopped her. "Did you hear that?" she whispered.

"Yeah. Stay here." He put his hand on her arm and actually felt it when she was about to argue. "I mean it, Haley."

"Be careful, Marlon."

He nodded, then rolled to a standing position and soundlessly moved to the doorway and peeked into the storeroom. A shape was backlit by outside lights in the open door. Marlon ducked back and waited in the main room for the guy to move past him. When he did, Marlon grabbed him from behind.

"Hey, man—"

One of the lamps switched on and Marlon blinked against the brightness, but didn't loosen his hold. "Haley, call the cops."

"He's just a kid, Marlon."

"I didn't know anyone was here." The young voice cracked with the pleading tone. "Let me go. I won't bother you again."

"Don't hurt him," Haley said.

"Hurt him?" This jerk had spoiled a day that should have been happy for her. And all she could think about was not hurting this kid who had no respect for locks and rules? "Are you serious?"

"Look at him. He's more scared than we are." She moved closer. "What's your name?"

There was no sound except heavy breathing from the exertion of their recent scuffle. Marlon tightened his arms, just a little pressure to give the aspiring delinquent something to think about.

"The lady asked you a question."

"Roy. Robbins," he added.

Marlon eased his grip and dropped his hands, then moved to the side to get a good look. Haley was right. He was just a kid, about sixteen or seventeen. Looked like a young Brad Pitt, but skinny and not much taller than Haley.

"What's your deal, kid?"

"None of your business."

"That's where you're wrong. When you broke in here and scared Haley it became my business." He glanced at the woman in question, who was looking back at him like an alien had popped out of his chest. "Do you know him?"

She shook her head. "You need help, don't you, Roy?" There was no answer, which spoke volumes. "The thing is, kiddo, you didn't need to break in. But you picked the right place. ROOTS is all about helping kids in trouble."

"I'm not in trouble—"

"Wrong again, kid." Marlon watched him closely, waiting for any movement that would indicate he was planning to run for it. "Breaking and entering is a crime. Call the cops, Haley," he said again.

"It's not necessary."

"How can you say that?" Marlon demanded.

"He's just a kid. Probably a runaway. Not dangerous. The authorities have enough to do. This isn't something we need to generate a lot of paperwork for. When my brother was about the same age, he ran away and I was frantic." She looked at the kid. "Let me call your parents to come get you."

"No way." Testosterone-fueled anger wrapped around the words.

"Your mom and dad are probably worried sick about you, Roy."

"They could give a crap," he said bitterly.

Haley frowned. "Did they hurt you?"

"It's not like that," he said quickly.

"Tell me what it's like," she urged.

The kid ran his fingers through his short, spiky, dirty-blond hair. "I just had to get out of there."

"To clear your head?" Haley asked.

"I guess." He lifted a thin shoulder.

Marlon was impressed that she seemed to get him, to understand a guy's need to be alone. Maybe she would comprehend his own need for speed and the resulting community service.

"Go ahead. Call the cops," Roy challenged, his voice sullen and resigned.

It grated on Marlon, but Haley just smiled.

"I don't think that's necessary," she said again. "I'm glad you weren't out on the street. You just needed a place to spend the night."

"And that justifies breaking and entering?" Marlon demanded.

"He didn't take anything."

"That's because you didn't have beer in the fridge," Marlon said wryly.

"That wasn't the best choice you could have made," Haley gently chided the teen.

Roy just shrugged. "Can I go now?"

"Do you have a place to sleep?" she asked, knowing full well he didn't or he wouldn't be here.

"What do you care?" the teen asked.

"That's not an answer." Haley folded her arms over her chest. "I'd give you permission to sleep here except my permit doesn't allow anyone under age to be here without adult supervision."

"Then I'll split and find somewhere else to crash."

Haley sighed. "Look, it's late. I'm tired. And I won't sleep if I'm worried about you."

Hey, Marlon thought, that was his line. He didn't like where this was heading.

"You don't have to," the kid told her.

"Doesn't mean I won't. You can come home with me."

"What?" Marlon stared at her and wondered if her bleeding heart was starving her brain of oxygen. "That's crazy. What do you know about him?"

"He's in trouble. That's all I need to know." She held up her hand to stop him when Roy started to deny it. "He reminds me of Austin when he was that age. It's why I started this program. How can I turn away the first kid who needs help? Where would my brother be if he'd been turned away when he needed it?"

"But, Haley—" Marlon met her stubborn gaze and slid the kid a wary look while trying to think of something to change her mind. "He's a total stranger. Bad things happen, even in Thunder Canyon."

"No one knows that better than me."

"Look, I didn't mean to—"

"Don't worry about it. The thing is, I'm a pretty good judge of character," she insisted. "And, if you're worried, you can follow me home."

No, he really couldn't. Not legally. "I don't have a car," he hedged.

"No wheels?" the kid said. "That's harsh."

"I didn't think I'd need any," he defended. "And if I did, I could borrow a truck from my dad's construction company."

"Well, I don't want to drive you back to town just because you have big-city induced trust issues," she said.

"I'll sleep on your couch."

She glared at him for several moments, then nodded, apparently getting the message that he wasn't backing down. "Roy can sleep on an air mattress in Austin's room."

"Okay."

That was a lie, Marlon thought, because nothing was okay. A night on her couch was the last thing he wanted but he couldn't let her drive out to her place all alone with a kid she didn't know anything about, and a runaway to boot. Damn this protective feeling. It was darned inconvenient.

It wasn't bad enough that he'd sat in the dark with her for hours, wanting to kiss her. Now he'd be spending the night under her roof.

On the other hand, it was the least he could do. She didn't just talk the talk. She walked the walk and was willing to put herself out there to help a kid in need. She was a really good person in addition to that sweet, sexy thing she had going on. She wasn't a taker, but a giver and for reasons he couldn't put his finger on, he found that incredibly appealing.

Marlon had a feeling he wouldn't actually get any sleep on her couch—and it had nothing to do with whether or not it was comfortable. Spending the night under the fascinating do-gooder's roof would give him ideas that would test a saint's willpower.

And he was no saint.

Chapter Four

The next morning, Haley sat in a booth at The Hitching Post next to Marlon, with Roy across from them. This place, with its cowboy ambience and distressed hardwood floors, was home away from home to her. Manager Linda Powell had given her a job when she badly needed one and that bought a lot of loyalty.

Since no wall separated the restaurant side from the bar side, she was glad that Roy's back was to it. Over the original bar from the 1880s saloon was a picture of owner Lily Divine wearing nothing but gauzy fabric strategically placed to keep her from being completely indecent. There was a better than even chance the teen had seen nude female pictures before, but it wasn't happening on Haley's watch.

She would have fed these two at her house, but cold cereal and toast were not the sort of comfort foods to inspire a troubled teen to loosen his tongue. Breakfast here where she worked was the plan because she'd heard that the way to a man's heart was through his stomach.

Marlon chose that moment to shift and brush his shoulder against hers and the resulting heat shooting through her made her wonder if the saying was true. Not that she wanted his heart—she didn't. She wasn't even sure she liked him, let alone trusted him. Besides, something bothered her about his explanation for not having a car. And why was he really helping at ROOTS?

But none of those questions stopped the heat from pooling in her belly when he brushed against her again. He smelled good, clean and manly. After they'd arrived this morning he'd gone upstairs to his apartment to clean up. She hadn't expected him to come back, but he'd surprised her. The two guys had eaten a full breakfast—eggs, bacon, hash browns and pancakes—but she'd lost her appetite the moment Marlon slid into the booth beside her.

The waitress on duty stopped by the booth with a pot of coffee in her hand. "I hope you enjoyed your breakfast?"

"Best pancakes I've ever had," Marlon said.

"Everything was really good, Shirley," Haley added, glancing at the teen who didn't look up. When he ordered coffee, she'd started to overrule him as being too young. Marlon touched her thigh, just a warning gesture that trapped her protest in her throat. She would never be sure whether she let it slide because being a guy Marlon knew more about guys, or simply that the sizzle generated by his touch zapped it from her mind.

Shirley Echols was a green-eyed redhead who'd grown up in Thunder Canyon. She went away to college, but came back every summer to work. Holding up the coffee pot she said, "Warm up?"

Haley shook her head as her two companions slid their mugs closer for refills, then remembered that this was the other girl's last day. "It's been great working with you this summer."

"Yeah. Me, too. I'll miss you."

"Where are you going?" Marlon asked.

"Back to college. UCLA. Senior year, finally."

"It's a great school," he said approvingly. "And Westwood is a nice area. Close to L.A., Hollywood, Santa Monica. The ocean. Some happening places."

"I know." Shirley slid him a flirty little smile.

Haley was suddenly less concerned about losing a coworker and covering those shifts than the fact that she didn't like the way Marlon was returning the smile. It could be that a sense of nagging envy was responsible. The two of them shared knowledge of a place Haley had never been and had no expectation of ever going. She was a hick who'd never been out of Montana and had no business wondering if the way to Marlon's heart was through his stomach. Or anything else about him, for that matter.

But darn it, what she was feeling seemed a lot like jealousy. Not that she'd had much experience with the emotion what with her lack of any dating history, but she couldn't deny that resentful pretty well described the knot in her stomach. She wasn't proud of it, but wouldn't deny it, either.

She might be a hick, but she was a polite hick. "Good luck with your last year of school."

"Thanks." Shirley started to walk away then said over her shoulder, "If you need anything else, let me know."

"Count on it," Marlon said with a wink.

Haley bit back a retort because it wasn't any of her business. But the boy across from her was. If she was going to help him, she had to get him to talk.

"Okay, Roy, so tell me again where you're from."

"I never said." He slouched lower in the seat, his empty plate in front of him.

"It was worth a shot." She tried to think of something to draw him out. "What brought you to Thunder Canyon?"

"The trucker I hitched a ride with."

The whole scenario sent a chill through her. "Taking rides from total strangers isn't very safe."

"Really?" Marlon's tone oozed sarcasm. "Carting around complete strangers isn't what smart, savvy people do?"

"I wouldn't hurt her," Roy said.

"I'd like to believe that." Marlon leaned back in the booth. "But you won't tell us more than your name. We don't have any way to check out that you're telling us the truth. Smart money is on keeping you under surveillance."

"He's just a kid," Haley protested. "Cut him some slack."

"Yeah," Roy chimed in. "You don't understand anything."

"So tell us about yourself." Haley wrapped her hands around her mug. "What grade are you in?"

He thought for a moment and apparently decided sharing that couldn't give too much away. "Twelfth."

"So you'll be a senior," she confirmed. "Last year of high school. Graduation. Prom."

"No way." He looked more sullen if possible.

"Do you play sports?" she asked.

"Some."

"I was on the football team in high school," Marlon shared.

Roy folded his arms over his chest. "Big deal."

It was to Haley. She remembered watching him play. If there was a girl at Thunder Canyon High who didn't have a crush on him, she didn't know her. She'd quietly observed him on the field and in the halls, wishing he'd notice her, but half afraid that if he did, she'd make a fool of herself. And then he'd kissed her, just a freak encounter at a football fund-raiser the summer after she graduated and he was home from college.

He'd kissed her and she was foolish enough to believe that the earth actually tilted for both of them when he promised to call her. When he never did, she realized that the earth only moved for her and felt like the worst kind of fool—the lovesick kind.

Fool me once, shame on you. Fool me twice, shame on me, she thought.

"Are you on a team?" she asked Roy.

"Football," he confirmed. "And basketball."

"Does your high school play Thunder Canyon during the season?" That information might narrow down where he lived.

"Maybe. Maybe not."

"Nice try, Haley," Marlon said.

"You can't trick me into telling you anything," the kid said. "Everything sucks and I'm not going back."

"What about your family?" she asked. "Your parents?"

When he didn't answer, Marlon said, "You do have parents?"

A sullen look slid over the teen's painfully young face. "Maybe. Maybe not."

Marlon rested his forearms on the table and studied the boy.

"Your parents probably care about you."

"Didn't say I had any."

"Assuming you do, they're probably worried. Although if it were up to me I'd be pretty ticked off at ungrateful offspring like you."

"Whatever. I can take care of myself."

"I'm sure you can," Haley agreed. "But when you care about someone, you worry."

"Who says I care about anyone but myself?" the teen argued.

"It's pretty clear you don't," Marlon snapped. "The least you can do is call them."

"Why should I? They don't care."

"So that would be a confirmation on having parents." Marlon nodded with satisfaction.

"I didn't say that," Roy said quickly.

"No one here is buying it. You need to let them know you're okay."

"Not gonna happen."

"Roy, they must be so worried. If I didn't know where my brother or sister was, I would be frantic."

"It's not like that where I come from."

"Someone cares enough to pay big bucks for the jeans and T-shirt you're wearing," Marlon pointed out. "Isn't that the MC/TC brand?"

"So?"

"It's expensive."

He should know, Haley thought. It was his. "I agree with Marlon."

"You do?" Marlon sounded shocked.

She glanced at his half-amused, half-surprised expression. "Yes, I do. Roy, you have to call your folks and let them know you're not dumped by the side of the road. Or starving. Or sick."

"You can't make me."

True. Now what was she going to do? Try to reason with him. But so far that hadn't worked. She could threaten, refuse to help unless he cooperated. But it wasn't a good idea to make threats you weren't prepared to follow through on. She couldn't turn him out in the cold. And she wasn't quite ready to go to the cops and see if anyone reported him missing. He might just run away again and not be lucky enough to find help.

Marlon blew out a breath. "Okay, tough guy. How about a shoot-out?"

Haley nearly got whiplash when she turned

to look at him. "What? You think pistols at ten paces will get the truth out of him?"

"Not guns. Basketball," he explained. "One on one."

"I'd kick your ass," Roy scoffed.

"Really?" Marlon nodded. "Okay, how about this. If you beat me I get Haley to back off."

What? She didn't like where this was going. "Wait a minute—"

He held up a hand to stop her. "If I win, you call the folks and let them know you're alive and well."

Doubt flickered around the edges of his bravado. "I don't know—"

"Just what I thought. No guts."

"Says who?"

Haley could almost see the testosterone arcing back and forth but wasn't so sure this was the way to get information.

"Look, kid," Marlon said, "You've got a big mouth, but so far I haven't seen anything to back it up. What have you got to lose?"

"Nothing." Blue eyes flashed with anger. "You're on. It should be easy to beat an old guy like you."

"Old?"

Haley felt him tense and saw his outraged

expression, which was hilarious. She couldn't stop the laughter that bubbled up. "Who knew that at twenty-five you were over the hill?"

"You're only a year behind me," he grumbled. "It won't be so funny three-hundred-and-sixty-five days from now."

Probably not, she thought. But it wasn't often the legendary Marlon Cates looked like he did now, and she planned to enjoy the experience while it lasted.

Marlon couldn't wait to tell Haley that the "old guy" was victorious. He and Roy were at ROOTS, hanging out inside after unlocking the door with the key she'd given him. He grabbed two cold sodas from the refrigerator and handed one to the kid who was sitting on the old sofa, humbled and quiet.

"Gotta work on your jump shot, kid," he said.

"Whatever." The tone attempted defiance and failed miserably. He took the soda, popped the top, and downed at least half in one long drink.

Marlon did the same, then looked around. This place was taking shape. The mural was nearly finished—Haley had outdone herself.

The wall depicted teens listening to music, playing video games, typing on the computer, reading books. She'd drawn a boy with braces on his teeth, a girl with a zit on her cheek, groups of kids talking.

In every scene, Haley had captured a reality and warmth that were emotionally true. They said writers had a "voice," and looking at her talented depiction of the teen world, it occurred to him that artists did too. He could see her sweetness, caring and sense of humor in every brush stroke on the wall.

The front door opened and in walked the artist herself, looking young enough to pass for one of the teenagers she was so passionate about helping. If she had makeup on, he couldn't tell. But that didn't make her any less beautiful. In fact, she was more lovely, more appealing than high-profile models and actresses all over L.A. and Hollywood because of her naturalness.

Her shiny brown hair was pulled into a ponytail and wisps of bangs teased her forehead. Her Hitching Post knit shirt, green this time, was tucked into a pair of jeans without any label, but the inexpensive denim hugged her hips and legs and made his fingers itch to cup her curves.

"Hey," she said, looking from him to the teen on the couch. The basketball was at his feet. "Well?"

Marlon grinned. "Old guys rule."

"You won?" She moved farther into the room, a shocked expression on her face.

"Don't sound so surprised."

"I'm surprised," Roy mumbled.

"I can't believe it," she said.

Roy leaned his elbows on skinny knees. "He got lucky."

Marlon happened to be looking into Haley's shining brown eyes and couldn't help thinking about a different kind of lucky. Then he pushed the thought away. She wasn't the type of girl a guy casually played around with, which made him a jerk for even thinking it. But he was also a guy and couldn't help wondering what it would be like to touch her....

"I'm very impressed," she said, then looked intently at Roy. "And have you held up your end of the bargain?"

"I was sort of hoping you'd let me scrub floors and toilets instead." There was a pleading expression in his eyes.

She shook her head. "Not a chance. Phone home."

"I'm not telling them where I am," he said stubbornly.

"No one says you have to. The deal was you let them know you're okay. Do you want to use my cell?"

"No. I don't want them tracking me."

Marlon leaned his forearms on the back of the recliner. "Unless they work for an elite law enforcement agency and are expecting your call, I don't think they can triangulate your position."

"Very funny," Roy said, but he was fighting a smile.

"I thought so."

"I'm waiting." Haley crossed her arms over her chest.

The teen huffed out a breath, then pulled out his phone and thumbed through his address book and hit dial. He waited and they could all hear when a woman answered.

"Ma? It's me. I'm fine. That's all I wanted to say." He rolled his eyes, then interrupted, "No. All you need to know is that I'm okay. Tell Dad whatever you want." Without another word he hung up. He finished his Coke, set the can on the coffee table, then grabbed the basketball and stood. "I'm going to shoot some hoops."

"You forgot something." Haley nodded at the empty can.

"There's a recycle container in the back room. Rule number one is pick up after yourself."

He rolled his eyes, huffed out another breath then grudgingly did as instructed. Then he walked to the front door and said, "Now can I go?"

"You need the practice," Marlon commented.

"Yes, you can go," Haley said.

Without another word, shrug, eye-rolling or huffing breath, Roy was gone.

Haley set her purse on the coffee table. "You didn't have to rub it in."

"Yeah, I really did."

"Because of the 'old guy' crack?" Her full lips curved up at the corners.

"Pretty much. Although, just between you and me, he almost beat me. In the end, it was experience that gave me the edge. That, and a killer jump shot."

"So you won because you're old?" she asked.

"No. I'm experienced."

"And vain."

He thought about that. "Maybe. But did he

have it coming? Oh, yeah. The kid needed to be taken down a peg or two. Humility is a building block of respect."

"What about his self-esteem?"

"What about mine?" he countered.

"You're an adult. You should be above that sort of thing."

"Call me shallow, but I felt the need to teach him a lesson. And, contrary to what most do-gooders—excluding yourself, of course —would have you believe, self-esteem isn't shaped by everyone telling you how wonderful you are. It's formed by putting in the work. You earn it by putting one foot in front of the other, day after day. Running away from your problems doesn't solve them. They just trot right along after you."

She tilted her head to the side as she studied him. The ends of her ponytail teased her shoulder and gave him more ideas a guy shouldn't have about a girl like her.

"What?" he asked warily.

"Is it possible I was wrong about you?"

That was unexpected. He shook his head. "I think there's a problem with my hearing."

"Why?"

"I could have sworn you said you were wrong about me."

"No." She fought a smile. "I said it was possible."

"Same thing." When she opened her mouth to protest, he held up a hand to stop her. "What is it you were wrong about?"

One of her eyebrows rose questioningly. "I never would have guessed that self-esteem was one of your issues."

"Humor me."

"Okay." She sighed. "Maybe I was wrong about a bad boy like you being able to relate to kids."

"Wow. And?"

"And what?"

"You questioned my role model qualifications," he reminded her.

"I was wrong. Seriously, Marlon, I understand now what you meant when you were talking about thinking outside the box. Roy never would have called his mom because I asked him to. You were right about understanding a guy's point of view. It never would have occurred to me to challenge him to one-on-one basketball, let alone be able to beat him. I'm sorry for misjudging you."

"Apology accepted."

"I'll go even further. Maybe—" she held up a finger in mock warning "—just maybe, you're a good man and actually as sincere as you seem."

When she smiled at him with genuine warmth and admiration, Marlon felt something shift and tighten in his chest. He'd vowed to get her respect. Mission accomplished. Having it felt even better and more satisfying than he'd expected. It was way past time to confess the real reason he was volunteering and assure her that he would do every last hour of his community service.

He straightened away from the chair and moved in front of her. "There's something I need to tell you—"

Music coming from her purse interrupted him. "My cell."

It took her a few seconds to rummage through her pocketbook before finding the phone. She flipped it open. "Hello. Hi, Linda. Sure, I can come in and help train the new girl. No problem. See you later." She hung up and looked at him. "Sorry. You were saying?"

"About why I wanted to give you a hand with this program—"

Just then the front door opened and a guy in postal service light blue shirt and gray-blue shorts walked in. "Hi, Haley."

"Hey, Bob. What's up?"

"I have something for you. Addressed to ROOTS."

She smiled. "My first mail here."

He handed her a packet. "It's from the Thunder Canyon Justice Center. The county clerk requires a signature."

"This makes me feel official," she said.

It made Marlon feel like crap. He had a pretty good idea what was inside. He watched her sign and hated that her first official mail for her pet project was about him and not in a good way.

When they were alone again, she ripped open the envelope before he could stop her.

"Haley, there's something I need to say—" But the words stuck in his throat when she looked up from the letter and the joy drained from her face, followed closely by the respect and admiration that had been there just moments ago.

"You had your license revoked for reckless driving," she accused.

"It wasn't exactly reckless. I was in complete control of my vehicle."

"And driving way over the speed limit."

"That's what I was trying to tell you," he said.

"So wanting to help the kids was a lie."

"Not exactly. I really do want to help them."

"Only so you can get your license reinstated. Not because you care." The warmth in her eyes was replaced by anger and disappointment.

He missed the warmth. "Yes, but—"

"But nothing. It's just like you said. You know all about trying to get away with stuff. Maybe you should try the truth for a change."

"Haley, you have to listen to me."

"No, I really don't." She shook her head and for a split second the sheen of tears glistened in her eyes. "My responsibility is to the teenagers who come here. I won't tolerate lies from them or anyone who's around them. You're fired, Marlon. Please leave."

He was a salesman and knew when to push and when to exit quietly. He chose the latter and walked out, closing the door behind him.

Losing an account had never felt as bad as this. He'd gone from hero to zero in a heartbeat. For one shining moment she'd admired how he handled the kid. He liked having her good opinion.

And he wanted it back.

He hadn't achieved success in the retail

market by going quietly and he wouldn't do it now. Not because it was about community service.

Now it was personal.

Chapter Five

She'd fired Marlon, but Haley was the one who was hot. Even several hours later during her lunch shift at The Hitching Post, she was mad. He'd had her snowed for about thirty seconds before she found out he couldn't be trusted. That must be a world record and a definite warning not to buy into his charm. Clearly she'd been wrong—he hadn't changed at all.

"I'm so stupid," she mumbled, distractedly setting a hamburger and fries down in front of Ben Walters.

"Hey. Whoa."

She stopped. "Did you need something else?"

"Yeah." He pointed to the seat on the other side of the table across from him. "Sit."

She sat. She never said no to Ben Walters, and not just because there weren't any thanks big enough for his support after her mom died. He was a big bear of a man with a thick barrel chest, pale blue eyes that saw too much, and gray hair. A widower in his mid-fifties, he had a deep voice and no tolerance for attitude. He was also her friend and she loved him very much.

He came to The Hitching Post nearly every day for breakfast, lunch or dinner. Sometimes all three. And always sat in the same place. In fact, they called it "Ben's booth", the one with an unobstructed view of Lily Divine over the bar.

Was it only a couple hours ago that she'd sat close by with Marlon and Roy, fretting about the teen seeing the nearly naked picture?

Ben unscrewed the top from the ketchup bottle, turned it upside down and hit the side with his huge palm until his fries were barely visible through the mound of red. "Tell me what's bothering you."

"Nothing."

His gaze jumped to hers. "So you look mad

enough to spit and call yourself names over nothing? I never knew you to tell fibs."

That stung. It put her in the same column as that fibbing Marlon Cates. "Okay, you're right. I'm ticked off at someone."

"Who?"

"Marlon Cates."

"Heard he was in town." Ben took a bite of his burger and held her gaze.

Haley hadn't planned to bore him with details, but they just came pouring out. "He claimed he wanted to help me with ROOTS."

"That's disturbing."

"I know. The thing is, I couldn't figure out why he would volunteer."

"Doesn't sound like him," Ben agreed.

"Turns out he got his third speeding ticket in a year and his license was revoked. The judge gave him community service and he's doing it at ROOTS. But he neglected to tell me that so I fired him."

Ben's ruddy face grew redder. "That kid was always wild. I knew way back when that he was trouble."

"No kidding."

"Nothing he's done since high school has changed my mind." He picked up the napkin and wiped his mouth. "Although he seems to have a head for business. That company of his turned out pretty well. They say he's worth millions."

"That's what they say," she agreed.

"Who knew jeans and western type stuff were worth so much?" He shook his head. "Always said Marlon Cates had a sales personality and it wasn't necessarily a compliment."

"It's a good thing he's successful," she said. "He can afford to pay his speeding tickets."

Ben nodded and finished chewing. "Did you hear about the time a few years back that he and his twin, Matt, got engaged to twin girls?"

"Yeah." As much as Haley wanted to ignore Marlon Cates talk, in a small town stories spread like the flu. "I heard his parents put a stop to it in a nanosecond."

Ben grinned. "Scandal sticks to that boy like white on rice. Since Thunder Canyon resort opened, if he was around, some Hollywood 'it' girl was always hot on his heels."

The reminder pricked a part of Haley that she thought was buried much deeper. "For sure his scandalous escapades border on urban legend here in Thunder Canyon."

"True enough," Ben said. "Good for you, booting his butt out of your place."

"In all fairness, he did help me with the heavy work. I'm not sure how I'd have moved the fridge and furniture without him."

"He's got an angle—"

Linda Powell, the Hitching Post manager, stopped by the table. "Who are you bad-mouthing now, Ben Walters?"

"No one who doesn't deserve it," Ben said. His blue eyes twinkled at the dark-haired woman and she smiled back, a decidedly flirtatious expression in her green eyes.

Haley noticed the attractive, dark blond-haired young woman beside her boss. She'd seen her in here before, but they hadn't met yet. Clearly that was about to change.

"Haley," Linda said, "I'd like to introduce Erin Castro."

"Nice to meet you, Erin." Haley held out her hand and the other woman shook it.

There was something about her that Haley couldn't really define. It had nothing to do with looks, because Erin was really pretty. Her worn jeans and white T-shirt, if anything, were simple and did not draw attention to how beautiful she was, even with her long hair pulled back into a simple ponytail. But there was a needy expression in her blue eyes.

It was just a feeling but if anyone knew what needy felt like it was Haley. Kindhearted people in this community had pulled her family through the worst time that anyone could imagine. She knew from experience that compassion was always appreciated.

Linda tucked a strand of shoulder-length hair behind her ear. "I just hired Erin to replace Shirley."

"Welcome to The Hitching Post family," Haley said. So this was the new girl she was going to help train. "Meet Ben Walters, my friend and one of our best customers."

"I like my burger medium well." His voice was friendly-gruff.

"Just write 'hockey puck' on the ticket and the cook will know who it's for," Linda teased.

"Thanks for the tip," Erin said.

"I haven't given you one yet." Ben studied her intently. "Gotta see how the service is first."

"Don't be mean, Ben," Linda said.

"Not mean. It's the God's honest truth."

"That's good," Erin said. "I'd rather have the truth than live with a lie."

Haley noticed a spark of intensity in the words, but chalked it up to nerves starting a new job. "Have you ever waitressed before, Erin?"

"I'm so grateful for this opportunity. Linda is taking a chance on me and I'll work hard not to let her down," she said, not really answering. "How long have you lived in Thunder Canyon, Haley?"

Haley noticed the one-hundred-eighty-degree turn away from herself, but didn't point it out. Instead she responded truthfully. "All my life. I grew up here."

"Wow, you must know everyone in town." Erin toyed with the end of her ponytail.

"I know a lot of people," Haley said.

"We were just talking about one of them when you walked up," Ben said. "That Marlon Cates is a piece of work."

"I haven't met him. Do you know him well?" Erin asked her, that edge of intensity slipping into her tone again.

If kissing him meant she knew him well, Haley did. But that wasn't something she was willing to share with her friends, let alone a stranger. "He was a year ahead of me in high school."

"Stay away from that one," Ben warned.

"Why?" Erin asked.

"He's not so bad," Linda chimed in. "Just a high-energy person."

"You call it high energy," Ben said frowning. "I call it bad news."

"Why?" Erin asked.

Haley didn't miss the girl's acute interest in Marlon and wondered about it, trying to ignore the sting of unwanted jealousy.

Another good reason for firing Marlon. He brought out the worst in her.

"It doesn't matter," Haley said. "He lives in Los Angeles and isn't staying in town long."

"I didn't mean to interrupt your lunch, Ben." Linda smiled. "Just wanted you both to meet the new girl."

"I look forward to working with you," Haley said honestly.

"Same here. Nice to meet you both."

As they walked away, Haley studied the newcomer's trim back and slender figure. She sure asked a lot of questions, but maybe it was an attempt at female bonding. Finding common ground for friendship.

The suspicious thoughts made her feel just the slightest bit hypocritical. After all, talk was the foundation of friendship. Talk was a way to communicate feelings. Haley had encouraged Roy to talk about what he was going through in an attempt to help.

Funny thing about talk. She'd just unburdened herself and didn't feel the least bit better for it. She was still bummed about firing her charming volunteer. She'd enjoyed spending time with him in spite of herself. But a lie of omission was still a lie.

The truth was that Marlon Cates hadn't changed at all. Ben was right about him being trouble. He was capable of breaking her heart without breaking his stride. Firing him was for the best. Her best.

Because she was starting to look forward to seeing him every day. And that wouldn't do her any good at all.

After a restless night dreaming about kissing Marlon, Haley drove into town with Roy. She had to work the breakfast shift at The Hitching Post, but couldn't order the teen to sit at a back table with some crayons and a coloring book to keep him out of trouble. As he pointedly said, he wasn't a baby and she wasn't his mother. She couldn't tell him what to do. After that he'd left and she hoped he was staying out of trouble.

There was a cockiness to Roy that reminded her of Marlon Cates, and she didn't mean that in a good way.

Apparently she had a weakness for bad boy charmers of all ages.

After her shift ended, she left her truck parked at work and walked over to ROOTS. The basics were there—TV, fridge, furniture. She'd hoped to have more on the walls, give the place a personality, but that would come eventually. School opening was still a few weeks away and a bad economy meant fewer jobs and more kids with time on their hands who needed a hangout.

She'd made some phone calls to Tori Jones and Allaire Traub, English and art teachers respectively at Thunder Canyon High School, and asked them to spread the word that ROOTS was open. Haley planned to spend every minute that she wasn't working or taking her own part-time college classes at her new venture.

Key in hand, she prepared to open the door, but then she looked in the window and saw a group of kids inside. But how did they get in? No one was supposed to be here without adult supervision.

Haley walked inside, struggling for calm. "Hi."

A chorus of four voices answered "hi" back. Roy was sitting on the sofa with Kim Wallace, a sixteen-year-old blue-eyed blonde. On the loveseat, C. J. McFarlane was rubbing shoulders with his best friend Jerilyn Doolin. Both of them were fifteen. He was a good-looking boy with auburn hair forever in need of a trim. A slender girl with dark hair and eyes, Jerilyn was dealing with her widower dad's drinking problem. The two kids hung out together and they made a cute couple. But she didn't want them to be a couple here at ROOTS without supervision.

"So, I see you've all met Roy," she said as casually as possible. She stared at the runaway and asked, "You didn't break in again, did you?"

"Nah. Marlon let us in."

Haley followed his look to the TV stand in the corner where the man in question had his broad back to the room and was dealing with what looked like a video game.

Marlon glanced over his shoulder. "Hi. I still have the key you gave me yesterday."

She'd completely forgotten. "I see."

He stood and walked over to stand beside her in front of the teenagers. "I ran into Roy this morning and we decided to come over here. Shoot some hoops. Watch TV. Hang out."

Would she have worried about the kid more or less if she'd known he was with Marlon? She would never know.

"Then C.J. and Jerilyn stopped by and he hooked us up," Roy said.

"And I was just walking by and saw them inside," Kim volunteered. "I needed to get out of the house."

"Why is that?" Marlon asked.

She tossed a long strand of blond hair over her shoulder. "My parents. They're fighting."

Haley's heart went out to the girl. "I'm sorry to hear that."

Kim squirmed on the sofa. "They're getting a divorce."

"Didn't I hear that your parents divorced, C.J.?" Marlon folded his arms over his wide chest as he looked down at the teens.

C.J. nodded. "It was hard."

Kim looked at him. "Did you get the 'we both love you but fell out of love with each other' speech?"

"Something like that," he agreed.

"I think the divorce manual has a chapter on how to talk to the kids." Kim looked sad and angry in equal parts. "If love has a short shelf life, why should I believe they won't decide not to love me?"

"A parent's relationship with a child is different than with each other," Marlon said. "It's unconditional."

"He's right," C.J. confirmed. "For a while my mom and dad were fighting over me. My mom sued him for full custody and was going to make me go to boarding school in Switzerland."

"Cool," Roy commented.

"That stinks," Kim and Jerilyn said together.

Haley remembered agreeing with Marlon about girls and boys thinking differently, and she'd just seen proof.

"What happened?" Marlon asked the teen.

"Mom's fiancé is all about family and made her see it wasn't a good idea to come between me and my dad, and they finally came together on what was best for me. I like it here in Thunder Canyon. Dad and Tori are getting married, which is cool." He shrugged. "It all worked out."

Kim didn't look convinced. "I can't see my mom coming around. She's driving me nuts. Has to know where I am every second. Calls my cell phone all the time. There are so many rules I can't even remember them all, let alone not break them."

"It's her way of trying to control an un- controllable situation." Marlon sat on the sofa beside her. "If she didn't love you, there wouldn't be any rules."

"Oh, please," Kim scoffed.

"Seriously. Think about it. If you break a rule, does she come down on you?"

"Like a manufactured home in a tornado," the girl confirmed. "I can't even remember how long I'm grounded for."

"I'm willing to bet your mom knows and will follow up. And don't you think it would be a lot easier for her to just let you do what- ever you want? Less work for her." He met her gaze. "That's what love is."

"I never thought about it like that," Kim admitted.

"A different perspective can be good." He stood and walked back over to the TV.

Who was this insightful man and what had he done with the real Marlon Cates? Haley wondered. It was all she could do not to let her mouth drop open. This was the first time she'd actually hung out with him. She'd seen him flirt and pick up women at the Hitching

Post and judged him harshly. He wasn't the one-dimensional man she'd thought.

Haley looked at the kids. "There are sodas in the fridge if anyone is thirsty."

"Cool," C.J. said.

They all mumbled agreement and went into the back room to check out the drink situation. Haley walked over to Marlon. "Could I have a word?"

"Of course. It's your place."

"That's right." When she was this close to him it was hard to think straight, let alone come up with words. "This is my place and I fired you yesterday."

He frowned thoughtfully. "Can you actually dismiss someone who's a volunteer?"

"Yes."

"But there's no salary involved. So there's nothing to keep me from just showing up." One corner of his mouth lifted and there was a twinkle in his brown eyes that made it awfully difficult to maintain the proper level of mad. "I really don't think you can terminate the services of a volunteer."

"Watch me."

"You're going to throw me out?" He looked down at her, drawing attention to the fact that he was bigger and stronger.

"Not personally," Haley said. "But I've got friends in town who can do it."

"So you're going to call in reinforcements?"

"If I have to," she confirmed.

"Even though I've got the legal system on my side?"

"Way to spin the bad stuff," she said. "Technically they're not on your side. It's community service and law abiding citizens don't get sentenced to it. You're bending the perception."

No surprise there. He excelled in bending perceptions along with rules.

"Look, Haley, I don't want to argue with you."

"Since when?"

And didn't that sound childish? She was a grown woman, but he made her feel like an insecure teenage girl. Her stomach fluttered, her legs barely held her up, and her palms were sweaty. It happened every time she was close to him and she didn't know what to do about that. So tossing him out seemed like a good idea and she was prepared to go to the mat on it.

"You've been arguing with me since you

came back to town. And doing it under false pretenses," she added.

"I was trying to tell you about the community service."

"Only because you knew I'd find out sooner or later," she accused.

"You're right."

"And because—" She blinked when his words sank in. "I am?"

He nodded. "I saw what you're doing here and it's a good thing. You're a good person. I didn't want you to think less of me." He pointed at her in warning. "And don't say that's not possible."

Her lips twitched as she suppressed a smile. "Okay."

"Now you know the truth. I'm here until I complete my service and get my license back. That should be the end of August. Basically I'm running MC/TC long distance by phone, fax and computer. Your free time is stretched to the limit. Mine is flexible. And there needs to be supervision for this place to be open."

"Adult supervision," she clarified.

"I guess speeding tickets cast some doubt, but I am of age." His expression turned wry. "Roy thinks I'm old."

"And you did convince him to hang out

here," she said grudgingly. "I suppose that's better than being at loose ends on the street and getting into trouble."

"See? I've already earned my keep." He slid an arm across her shoulders and pulled her against him. "Come on, Haley. We can help each other."

"Well," she said, thinking out loud. "That would mean ROOTS hours could be expanded during the last days of summer before school starts in September."

"See?" He hugged her closer. "You need me."

He was right. But she would never admit that in a million years, let alone say it out loud. "It's community service, Marlon. I'm doing you a favor."

"So that's a yes?"

"It is."

And she wasn't sure whether it was his logical debate or the feel of his warm, strong body next to hers that had tipped the scales in his favor. She really could not think straight when she was close to him. But she'd agreed and wouldn't take it back.

That didn't mean she had to like it—or him.

So she had to assume that liking wasn't

necessarily a prerequisite for attraction. Because if her hammering heart was anything to go by, she was more attracted to Marlon than ever. And she'd just said he could hang out here at ROOTS.

She'd be okay as long as he didn't kiss her.

Chapter Six

Marlon knew that anyone who wanted action on Friday night in Thunder Canyon could find it at The Hitching Post. This Friday was no exception and, while not really wanting action, it was more of a distraction. He was hanging out with three of his high school football buddies. Steady Eddie Stevens, Jimmy "Evil E" Evanson and Big Mike "Tuck" Tucker. They were in a corner at one of the bistro-style high tables and chairs, the best place to see the whole room. In the past he'd found that advantageous for scoping out women. But tonight there was only one woman he was looking for.

Haley.

He saw her weave between tables, taking orders and delivering drinks and food. She was both graceful and gorgeous. It ticked him off that she was the only one he wanted to look at.

He dragged his gaze away from her and glanced around the table at his friends. "So let's catch up. What's going on with you guys?"

"I'm getting ready to expand my business." Eddie used to be a wide receiver in high school—tall, wiry and fast. The darkhaired, blue-eyed athlete-turned-rancher had always been surrounded by girls. "I'll be taking in guests nine months of the year. In the summer it'll be a kids' camp."

"You're starting a dude ranch?" Marlon asked.

"It's still a working ranch," Eddie protested.

"And more," redheaded Jimmy said. He'd played on special teams. "The kids coming to the camp have been through some kind of trauma. It's going to be a special program."

"Sounds impressive."

"I'll still do what I do." Eddie shrugged. "Raise horses. But in this economy diversification is the best way to stay afloat."

"Can't argue with that." Marlon took a sip of his beer. A camp for traumatized kids was a good thing; Haley would approve. In fact, the two of them were probably made for each other, but that thought made him want to put his fist through a wall. "Sounds like a chick-magnet scenario."

"No way." Eddie's voice was emphatic. "Been there, done that. Sworn off for good. I'll never understand women and it's my experience that putting in the energy trying isn't worth the kick in the teeth you get out of it."

Marlon's eyebrows rose and he looked at the other two who appeared as clueless as himself. "Want to talk about it?"

"I'd rather chew off my arm."

"Okay, then. Moving on." He looked at Mike. The guy was built like a mountain, big and beefy with sandy brown hair and gray eyes. He'd been a defensive end when they played football and rarely did anyone get by him. "What about you?"

"Still with Cates Construction," he said wryly. "I'm working on the McFarlane place. Your dad's a good boss and when Matt takes over I don't expect anything will change."

Marlon made a mental note to talk to his twin about that. He figured his brother already knew he was expected to eventually run the business, but would check it out. "Anyone special in your life?"

"Stella Dunlay."

"The cheerleader?" Marlon asked.

"Yeah. We're each other's rebound relationship." He shrugged, slightly uncomfortable talking about the personal. "We're having fun. Nothing serious."

"Way to keep it light," Marlon agreed. Two down, one to go. He raised an eyebrow at Jimmy.

He was tall, muscular, good-natured and funny. All attributes that kept him from getting picked on because of his red hair. Now he taught science and math at Thunder Canyon High and coached the football team. "This is probably as good a time as any to announce that I'm getting married. Penny Carlson."

The other two guys looked as surprised as Marlon felt. But they regrouped, slapped him on the back, clinked their beer mugs in congratulations and drank to the good news.

"When?" Marlon asked.

"Soon. She's pregnant," he added. "I was going to ask her to marry me anyway, but the unexpected news sort of speeded up the timetable. We're happy about it."

He looked it, Marlon thought. So they slapped him on the back again, clinked glasses and congratulated him on more good news.

"You, with a wife and kid. I can't believe it," Marlon said.

Jimmy shrugged. "It's easy. I love her."

If the place wasn't dark, Marlon knew his friend's face would be as red as his hair. He couldn't ever remember talking about feelings with these guys. It was always babes, boobs and butts. Those were great memories, but he didn't miss the old days. They'd all grown up. And Jimmy was going to be a husband and father... Marlon felt a stab of envy and figured Roy was right about him being old.

Just then he spotted Haley across the room, balancing a tray with a pitcher of beer and four mugs. She smiled and charmingly set it all down for four guys he didn't know. Then one of them slid an arm around her waist and she smiled, making Marlon want to put his fist through a wall again. If he didn't get over whatever this was, he'd be generating a lot of drywall repair business for Cates Construction.

"Earth to Marlon."

He looked at Mike. "Did you say something?"

"Yeah." The big guy followed his look and nodded knowingly. "So what's up with you?"

"Same old, same old."

"If that were true," Jimmy said, "the women of Thunder Canyon would be looking at the dust your car kicked up on the way out of town. Yet here you sit. Don't take this the wrong way, but why are you still here?"

"He's right." Eddie drained the last of the beer in his glass. "What's up with you?"

"Everything okay with your family?" Jimmy asked. Mr. Sensitive.

"Yeah. They're all good."

"Then I don't get it. Especially the part where you're working at Haley Anderson's teen program," Mike said.

You had to love small towns. Of course news of him at ROOTS would spread. Haley knew the worst so there was no point in blowing off his friends.

"Okay. You got me. Here's the short version. One too many speeding tickets got my license revoked and a month of community service. I'm doing it at ROOTS and when it's over at the end of August, I get my license back."

"And you're outta here." Jimmy wasn't asking.

"Yeah. I'm gone."

The declaration had him searching the crowded place for Haley. She was leaning over the bar talking to the bartender. With her brown, silky hair swept up in a pony-tail, she didn't look old enough to drink li-quor, let alone serve it. Her full mouth curved into a dazzling smile that he wished was for him, and his palms itched to cup her hips and pull her against him. But that wasn't likely to happen since she had no respect for him and thought commitment wasn't his strength.

He looked at his friends. "Yeah, I'll be outta here."

"Then we need to have another round while we can." Eddie held up a hand to get Haley's attention.

Seconds later she zigzagged through the maze of tables and stood beside Marlon, but looked at his friends. "What can I get you guys?"

"Another pitcher of beer," Mike said.

"Coming right up."

Marlon recognized the sweet fragrance of her skin, floating over the smell of burgers, fries and beer that permeated the place. It was like she had a special frequency just for him that teased his hormones. She wasn't more than an inch away and he could feel the heat of her body. Normally he looked down at her but the height of the table and chairs put them close, so close he would hardly need to move to touch his mouth to hers.

"This is like déjà vu all over again," Mike said.

"What the heck are you talking about?" Jimmy just asked what they were all thinking.

"It's like high school." The big guy grinned as if that explained it clearly.

Haley frowned. "I can't speak for anyone else, but I didn't drink beer in high school."

Of course she didn't, Marlon thought. She didn't break the rules. He found that incredibly appealing, especially when he remembered kissing her and the eager way she'd responded.

"You guys are missing the point," Mike complained.

"Because you haven't made one yet," the guys said together.

"Okay. I'll spell it out," the big guy said patiently. "Marlon, seeing you and Haley together reminds me of that high school football fundraiser. Remember?"

Jimmy snapped his fingers. "Yeah. It's the annual carnival. We had it last month. The kissing booth. It's still a big draw."

"Right," Eddie agreed. "I remember now. Haley was there taking tickets and Marlon kissed her. No one was ever sure quite how it happened, but we all said the two of you should get a room."

"That's right," Marlon said, pretending he just recalled the incident instead of thinking about it just minutes ago.

That was six years ago. He'd come home for the summer after his first year of college. The carnival was a big deal and he'd gone to support his former team. He'd thought Haley had volunteered to be the kissee. He'd handed her his ticket, pulled her close and kissed her until everything around them had disappeared.

He could still hear the breathless little moany noises she made and could still see the dazed expression on her face when they came up for air. Now all he saw in her expression was confusion with a little panic around the edges.

"I don't remember that," she said.

His friends hooted at him and Mike

grinned. "So the Marlon magic isn't as all powerful as we were led to believe."

"Seriously?" Marlon shifted away and studied her. "You don't recall that carnival?"

"Sure I do. It happens every year. But kissing you?" She shrugged. "Not so much."

"Ouch, buddy." Eddie's expression was dripping with pity.

"Not that it hasn't been fun walking down memory lane," she said looking around the table. "But I'll go get that pitcher now."

After she was gone, his friends hooted, hollered and continued to razz him about losing his touch with the ladies. The taunting wasn't what made him follow her. It was the fact that Miss-Play-By-The-Rules was lying through her beautiful, straight, white teeth.

At the bar, he reached out and took the circular tray away from her and set it down. When she started to protest, he grabbed her hand and tugged gently. "Come with me."

"I have stuff to do here," she protested.

"Take a break."

He took her out the back door to the parking lot filled with cars. "What the heck are you pulling?"

She yanked her hand away, then folded her

arms over her chest. "I have no idea what you're talking about."

"You don't remember kissing me?"

"No." Her chin lifted just a little higher but her gaze shifted off to the left.

"I don't believe you."

"Really? Why do you care that I don't remember? You're more into dating volume than substance. Once a heartbreaker, always a heartbreaker."

He ignored the dig and pointed at her. "I think you remember that kiss but you don't want to."

She made a scoffing sound. "Your ego is getting bigger by the second."

"So is your nose. You're lying, Haley. More to yourself than to me. You don't want to admit that there's something simmering between us."

"In your dreams," she denied.

He tapped her on the nose. "It's growing with every lie."

"I'm telling the truth," she protested.

"For someone who puts so much energy into sincerity, you've got a double standard going on."

"Oh, please. I've got work to do." She turned away and disappeared inside.

Marlon stared after her for a long time, then grinned. Her intense reaction all but confirmed his suspicions. If she didn't care about him, teasing would have been the go-to response. But it hadn't. She'd denied everything, then headed for high ground. Because she liked him.

That made him want to kiss her again, kiss her so thoroughly that if anyone saw the two of them locking lips they'd suggest getting a room. What would Miss-Play-By-The-Rules do if they did?

He wanted an answer to that question more every day.

The next day Haley still couldn't forget her conversation with Marlon the night before. She stacked dirty lunch dishes in a big, plastic rectangular container and took them into the back where Jeff, the teen Linda had hired for the summer, was waiting to load them into the industrial-sized washer. It kept her hands busy, but her mind kept going back to Marlon calling her a liar. Maybe starting ROOTS would cancel out the sin.

For every kid who found a job, there were a whole lot more with too much time on their hands and money worries on their minds. At least during these few weeks before school started and the teens would have homework, sports and activities to keep them busy, she'd managed to get ROOTS up and running.

And Marlon Cates had made that possible. MC—major crush. Still? She didn't want to believe it, but there was very little evidence to the contrary. Even worse, Marlon had noticed.

Walking from the kitchen back through the restaurant, she saw a familiar face. Carleigh Benedict from Thunder Canyon Social Services was sitting alone in a booth, holding her phone and probably looking at messages. Haley liked to think her tight-knit community was immune to the problems that were rampant in big cities, but that wasn't the case. Women and children were still abused and abandoned. Carleigh was far too busy and her time advising Haley about the youth center had been very much appreciated.

Haley stopped at the end of the table. "Hi, there."

The woman looked up and smiled. "Haley. I was hoping to see you. Are you busy?"

She shook her head. "Just finished my shift. Can I get you anything?"

"Someone just took my order. I don't re-member seeing her here before."

"She's new. Her name is Erin Castro."

"Very pretty," Carleigh commented.

And the new girl wasn't the only pretty one. Carleigh Benedict was a green-eyed blonde—sweet, smart and stunning. Everything Haley wasn't, but she liked the social worker anyway.

"Would you join me? I hate eating alone."

Haley was anxious to get to ROOTS, but Marlon was there to supervise the kids who'd stopped in. "Sure. I've got time for my favorite mentor. How ungrateful would I be to let you sit here by yourself?"

She slid onto the bench seat just as Erin delivered a Cobb salad, bleu cheese dressing on the side.

"Can I get you anything else?" Erin smiled automatically.

"Nothing, thanks," Carleigh answered.

"Okay, then." She looked at Haley. "My shift is over. See you tomorrow?"

"I'll be here." Haley watched the other woman walk away. What was her story? So far she'd been long on questions and short on personal details.

Carleigh dipped her fork into the dressing then speared some lettuce and egg. "So, I just came from ROOTS. It's really shaping up."

The social worker had been incredibly generous with her suggestions for dealing with the kids and setting down reasonable rules. She'd shared information on behaviors that were within normal teenage parameters, which ones to watch and when to get involved. Haley wished she'd had Carleigh when her brother was acting out after their mom died.

Haley smiled across the table. "It all came together really fast." Thanks to Marlon. Just thinking his name made her heart skip a beat and she tried to ignore it.

"The mural is terrific. Who did you get to do it?"

"Me."

Carleigh's eyes opened wide in surprise. When she finished chewing, she said, "You're pulling my leg. I had no idea you were so talented."

Haley shrugged off the compliment. "I've been taking art classes at the junior college."

"It shows." The other woman's gaze was intense and perceptive. "You really should think about a career in that field."

"I have thought about it."

"And?"

"It will never be more than a hobby." That

didn't stop her from thinking about it, though. "Creative endeavors are time-intensive without guarantee of any reward. I've got bills to pay and family to take care of."

Carleigh nodded. "I understand. But you're really good. Not that I'm an expert. But I know what I like."

"Thanks." Now let's change the subject, Haley thought.

"I met some of the kids while I was there," her friend said.

"Don't tell me. Roy. Kim. Jerilyn and C.J." The four had come in every day since that first time and seemed to enjoy hanging out.

"Yeah. Along with a few others. Seth. Ilene. Eric and Danielle."

"Word is spreading. They're checking out the new place. Boredom must be setting in after all these weeks of summer."

"Then your timing in getting it open is perfect. Imagine what they'd be doing if there was no ROOTS." Carleigh set her fork down for a moment. "I met Marlon Cates, too."

Just hearing his name made Haley's chest feel funny and she shifted to ease it. "Without him, the place couldn't be open until I got off work. It gives the kids more time to hang out with supervision."

"He told me about his community service."

Haley looked up quickly, hoping that wouldn't be a problem for her fledgling project. "He's just temporary. He won't be around long enough to have a negative effect on the kids."

"I'm not second-guessing your decision."

Haley wished she could say the same. Every time she saw him her heart beat too fast and she could barely breathe. That wasn't a neutral reaction when neutral was how she so desperately wanted to feel.

"No?" she asked.

Carleigh shook her head. "When I was there he was explaining to Seth why he was ordered by the court to do community service. He broke the rules and got caught. It's good for the kids to see someone taking their punishment like a man."

Man being the operative word. Broad shoulders, wide chest, strong arms, a face to make women sigh with longing. He was a man all right.

"I'm glad you think it's okay for him to be there."

"I definitely do." The other woman smiled. "We all make mistakes. No one is perfect. That doesn't mean you can't be successful.

Part of flourishing is being able to admit when you're wrong and take responsibility for your actions."

Haley blinked. "So you're saying he broke the law and is a good role model anyway?"

"I wouldn't exactly put those two thoughts together back to back without qualifying them," Carleigh explained. "But yes. If a mega-successful businessman like Marlon Cates isn't above answering to the law, what chance do teenagers have against it? He's rich, powerful and doing his time. It sends a very strong positive message. It's a good lesson for the kids."

Not just the kids, Haley thought. Marlon had tried to tell her he could give the teens a different point of view, but she hadn't really bought into it. Not until she'd seen him with Roy and the other kids. The truth was, she'd been looking for excuses to push him away in order to keep him from hurting her again. In the end, getting ROOTS open had to take priority over her feelings.

"He's been a big help," she admitted.

"Another plus is that he's not hard on the eyes." An appreciative smile curved up the corners of Carleigh's mouth.

Haley wasn't surprised when once again she felt a twinge of jealousy in her chest.

"I didn't notice," she lied.

"You're kidding, right?"

Haley's cheeks heated when she realized it was the second time in the last couple of days that she'd been caught. Marlon had seen through her when she'd claimed not to remember kissing him. In her mind, she could still picture that moment when their lips touched. It hadn't been her only kiss, but nothing else had even come close to the way Marlon had made her heart race and her body hum. And she had thought far too much about doing it again.

He'd said she wouldn't admit that there was something simmering between them, and he was right about that. She refused to let it be true. Even if it were, there was no point in admitting as much. It would just make everything harder when he was gone.

Now Carleigh accused her of not telling the truth. Was it still a lie if the person it was directed at didn't believe you?

"Okay. You're right. I have noticed. He's pretty cute."

"But?" Carleigh frowned.

"What makes you think there's a 'but'?"

"I can tell by the look on your face. What's wrong, Haley?"

"I like him."

Carleigh toyed with her paper napkin and started to shred it. "And that's bad…why?"

"Because it's not good," she hedged.

"Again I ask…why?"

"He's not staying. And even if he were, he's experienced with women."

"So?"

"I'm not. Experienced with men, I mean." She met the other woman's gaze and the words came tumbling out. "I was too busy studying in high school to date. Then I went away to college and met a guy. We were heading in that direction—"

"You mean sex?"

"Yeah." Again heat flared in her cheeks. "My mom always said I should wait, make sure I loved the person before taking the step."

"And did you?"

She shook her head. "I never had the chance. My mom was killed in the car accident and I came home to take care of Angie and Austin. That was the end of my college experience."

Carleigh knew her story, but the expression on her face was sympathetic. "And sex?"

Haley couldn't answer, just stared across the table, feeling the warmth of embarrassment creep up her neck.

"You've never had sex?" Carleigh asked, struggling unsuccessfully to act as if that didn't make Haley a mutant in this day and age.

"The technical term is virgin." She shrugged. "I've been raising my siblings and working. There's been no time, energy, or even a guy who interested me."

"Until now?" Carleigh's eyebrow rose questioningly.

Haley nodded miserably. "My lack of worldliness never bothered me before. But what if things between Marlon and me go there? What if he laughed at me?"

Carleigh was making a pile of white confetti with her napkin as she thought about what to say. "Can we agree that I'm a pretty good judge of character?"

Haley knew her friend saw all kinds of people and sized them up quickly and accurately. "Yes."

"Okay. I observed your Marlon interacting with those teenagers and did not see a man who would hurt a woman's feelings by laughing at her. He appeared to be sensitive, smart and insightful."

"Okay."

She looked at the watch on her wrist and sighed. "I've got to run. But let me leave you with this thought. Life is not a spectator sport."

True enough, thought Haley. But if one just observed there was little danger of getting beaned by a fastball. Status quo didn't rip your heart out or turn your life upside down. She knew how that felt and was determined to stay in status quo territory.

Marlon was right about her being the queen of denial, but that was okay with her, because he wasn't now and never would be her Marlon.

Chapter Seven

Marlon paced the length of his room above The Hitching Post for the umpteenth time. Fridays in Thunder Canyon were fun, but Monday night the place was dull as dirt. TV wasn't his thing and nine-thirty was too early to turn in. He knew the devil had a seat in hell with his name on it when thoughts of going to bed made him picture Haley lying by his side.

He walked to the window and lifted aside the lace covering for a better view of Main Street and ROOTS. Light from inside the teen center spilled onto the wooden walkway in front, which meant someone was there. It had to be her.

He'd only seen Haley for a few minutes earlier that day. She'd dropped into ROOTS a couple of times to check on things. Then she'd relieved him of duty after her shift at the bar and grill ended. Clearly she hadn't wanted to chat. The last time they had, he'd accused her of lying. He'd bet everything he owned that she remembered kissing him. And bringing it up with her earlier had been tempting, but with kids wandering in and out it wasn't appropriate.

Maybe she was alone now.

The thought was too tempting to resist. He left his room and went down the rear stairs, taking his usual back route to Main Street. There weren't a whole lot of folks around, but he didn't want to chance running across someone who felt like chatting him up. He wasn't in the mood for idle conversation. Only one brown-eyed girl was on his mind and he was pumped for a chat with her.

The dull thud of his boots sounded on the wooden sidewalk outside the teen center. He was right about her being here. Through the window Marlon could see her sitting on the sofa, with pencil in hand and a pad of paper on her lap. No one else was with her.

She was sketching something and looked

especially cute and far too appealing with her forehead furrowed in concentration. One foot was tucked up underneath her and she'd caught her bottom lip between her teeth.

He'd like to bite her bottom lip. Not hard. Just a nip, something to show her that thoughts of her mouth had cost him a decent night's sleep ever since that first day he'd seen her here working on the mural. He pushed open the door and decided leading with that particular revelation would not be the best way to go.

She looked up. "Marlon. What are you doing here?"

"I could ask you the same thing."

"This place is my project. What's your excuse?"

His punishment, he wanted to say. But he wasn't talking about legal obligations. Thoughts of her tortured him pretty much all the time.

He moved farther into the room, just on the other side of the coffee table. "I saw your light on. Isn't it kind of late?"

"Kids have been in and out all day. Because they're still on summer break it hasn't been quiet." She shrugged. "I'm keeping the place open until ten. Just in case someone wants to come by and talk."

As it happened, someone did want to talk, although he probably wasn't on her approved list. But it occurred to him, and not for the first time, how selfless her dedication was to this project. She was giving up a lot of precious personal time for the benefit of teens who didn't have much of a clue how hard she was working to make this happen.

"What?" she asked, eyes narrowing on him.

"Nothing." He sat down beside her. "I was just thinking."

"About?"

"Do the kids have any idea how much time, effort and sacrifice you've put in to make this place a reality for them?"

"Is that a rhetorical question?"

"Not really," he said.

"Too bad, because I really don't have an answer for you."

"Why do you do that?"

She looked up from her sketching. "What?"

"Make light of your efforts. This has been a time-consuming venture, and I'm sure it was frustrating at times. But you didn't give up and now ROOTS is a reality." He met her gaze. "You're a giver and I'm guessing it's not because you expect to get anything out of it. Most people would rather be home with their feet up."

"Wait a second." She tilted her head to look at him and the end of her ponytail brushed her slender shoulder. "Number one, don't make me out to be something I'm not. I get something out of this."

"What?"

"The satisfaction of giving back to the community."

He nodded. "If that was number one, there must be a number two. Care to share?"

"Right now all I'm doing is sitting here. It's exactly what I'd be doing at home. No big deal."

He leaned over to get a look. "What are you sitting here doing?"

"Sketching." Quickly she flipped the cover over her work. "Just doodling really."

"Looked like more than that to me." He reached out a hand to take the pad, but she hopped up and backed away.

"It's nothing."

"I'd like to see it." He stood and moved toward her.

"You don't have to be polite."

"I'm not. Trust me. It's genuine interest."

"Like I believe that. This is you we're talking about." But she put the sketch pad behind her back.

Marlon stared at her. "If I weren't so secure and self-confident, that dig might have hurt my feelings. But I'm pretty sure you're trying to pick a fight in an effort to distract me."

He moved closer until they were practically touching. Her eyes widened and the pulse in her neck fluttered wildly. While he had her where he wanted her, he reached around her and tried to snag the notebook.

They wrestled for several moments, her small firm breasts brushing against his chest. Now that almost distracted him but he persevered. In the end, it wasn't his superior strength that finally won out. He had his arms around her and they were both breathing hard. Her lips parted and her chest was rising and falling rapidly. It was either kiss her or take advantage of her guard being down.

The latter seemed a wiser choice and he easily grabbed the sketch pad from her limp fingers.

"Hey," she said. "That was cheating."

"Define cheating." When she didn't, he

continued. "I simply saw an opportunity and made my move."

But not the one he'd wanted most. And when she pressed her full lips together, he was pretty sure she felt the frustration, too. But he'd missed his chance with her after kissing her six years ago. He needed to let the whole thing go. Leaving town right now wasn't an option and when he finally did, he didn't want any regrets. While he was stuck, he couldn't make a move on her.

He turned around and started flipping through her notebook. She made several attempts to take back her work but he was taller and quicker, evading every grab. As he turned the pages and saw her sketches, something buzzed in his businessman's brain. The drawings were of jeans, shirts, jackets, scarves, and handbags. She didn't just use charcoal pencil, but colored ones as well. The purses especially caught his eye.

The designs had fringe, buckles, snaps and zippers. Inside, the lining was done in plaids, polka dots, and different patterns. Some had snowflakes. Horses. Saddles.

He looked at her. "These are really good, Haley."

"You're just saying that to make up for being a jerk."

"I'm not that nice."

"No kidding." Her look was wry.

"Seriously." He looked down at the sketches. "You're very talented."

"Now you're starting to scare me."

"Whatever your opinion is of me personally, I probably deserve," he said. "But when it comes to business success, I've earned that, too. I didn't take MC/TC to where it is by being an idiot. Or being nice. The fact is that I know talent when I see it. And these are very good ideas."

"Thanks." She blinked up at him. "So the company is doing well?"

"As well as can be expected in this economy. Well enough that I've had buyout offers and I'm considering them."

"You'd sell it?"

"I'm weighing the pros and cons."

"But you started it all by marketing your merchandise at D.J.'s Rib Shack at the resort," she reminded him. "I thought MC stood for Marlon Cates and TC is Thunder Canyon."

"It is," he admitted.

"Your company has local roots. I think that's worth holding on to."

A whole lot of heart was shining in her eyes and he couldn't say what he wanted to. Business was all about the bottom line. Sentiment didn't make a company worth fighting for. But as he studied her drawings his mind was going a mile a minute.

"MC/TC could use fresh and innovative products to give it new life and jump start sales. Your designs could do that." He didn't realize he'd said that out loud until she responded.

"That would be exciting."

His mind was still racing when he said, "Let me take you to dinner. We'll discuss the opportunity."

"I don't know." She slid her fingertips into the pockets of her worn jeans. "Who will be here at ROOTS?"

"You have to eat. Closing the door for an hour won't make a difference, will it?"

He wanted to take her out to dinner and business was probably the last reason on his list. This definitely went under the personal column. Sales were his thing and now he was selling himself.

"Maybe Austin would hang out here while you have a night off," he suggested.

"I hate to ask. He works hard at the resort and—"

"And you don't? Work hard, I mean." He handed back her notebook. "Isn't he the one who inspired this place? The one who saw the error of his ways because of community involvement? The one who's a college graduate because of it?"

"Yes, but—"

"If you don't ask him, I will. You're getting a night off and I'm not taking no for an answer."

She didn't look happy, but there was surrender in her eyes. "I'll work it out."

"Good. Tomorrow night. Seven o'clock."

"Okay."

Marlon nodded and walked out without another word. Never jeopardize the deal by talking too much after you got what you wanted. But grinning was allowed, which was good since he wasn't sure he could wipe the smile off his face.

Funny how things could change in a heartbeat. Just like that, he was looking forward to another night in Thunder Canyon.

Seemed like a good idea at the time. Caught up in the moment. What harm could it do?

All of the above described why Haley had agreed to dinner with Marlon. A simple No, thank you was what she wished she'd said last night when he'd asked. But she hadn't.

Now she was locking up ROOTS while he waited behind her to walk to The Hitching Post just down the street. Really, she decided, what could happen?

Taking a deep breath, she turned and smiled. "All secure."

"Good." Looking uncertain, he met her gaze. "Are you okay with The Hitching Post? You already spend most of your time there."

"It's fine." She knew everyone and would be among friends. It would help her relax, although she wasn't sure that was possible no matter where they went. "I have inside knowledge of just how good the food is there."

"When I get my driver's license back, I'll take you to a place where you don't know the kitchen like the back of your hand."

"It would probably be best if you didn't make promises."

She hadn't meant to sound so curt, but his track record in keeping them wasn't good. Granted it was just the one time, but that had been enough for her. She'd wasted a lot of time and energy waiting for a call that never came. It hurt a lot and she'd felt stupid for believing. That wasn't a feeling she wanted to repeat.

"Despite what you think, I can keep my word," he said quietly.

"I just meant," she said, "that you don't owe me anything. Let's just be in the moment and let tomorrow take care of itself."

He looked down at her for several moments, then finally said, "Okay."

"Okay." Their footsteps scraped on the wooden walkway and she kept trying to keep her distance as they walked. But somehow, with the uneven boards, she kept rubbing up against him. A brush of bare arms. Bumping her shoulder into his muscular biceps. The scent of his skin. The combination ganged up on her senses and made rational thought a challenge. Without coherent ideas conversation wasn't easy. But she'd do her best to soldier through.

"So tell me more about how your company works. What happens to sketches like mine?"

"My creative team looks at concepts with potential. When they find something that really gets their juices going, we meet with marketing and pinpoint our target demographic.

We evaluate the chances of success before pouring millions of dollars into a project."

She stopped in her tracks and stared up at him. "Excuse me, I could have sworn you just said millions."

"I did. First you have to come up with something people will want to have, then create that product. Labor, materials and marketing costs have to be paid before anything is even sold."

"So the saying is true. It really does take money to make money."

He nodded. "I got lucky in college with the MC/TC brand. There was a venue to display my product and someone with money was staying at Thunder Canyon Resort. He was looking for an investment and liked what he saw. The rest is history."

"That must be a lot of pressure. Putting capital into something without any guarantee that it will be successful."

"You learn to trust your instincts," he said. "Listen to the voice in your head, the feeling in your gut. When you see something you know it."

"And you saw something in my sketches?" She just couldn't believe her doodles could be turned into something profitable.

"They're original and imaginative, Haley."
He stopped suddenly and when she tripped on
an uneven board in the walkway, he curved
his fingers around her arm to steady her. "I
knew there was something the first time I
saw you—"

They stared at each other for what felt like
a lifetime and Haley couldn't breathe. Lights
along Main Street illuminated the intensity in
Marlon's dark eyes. What was he thinking?
What should she do?

Keep walking, that's what. It was hard to
hit a moving target.

But as her muscles tensed to take a step,
his fingers closed a little tighter, keeping her
right where she was. When he threaded the
fingers of his other hand into her loose hair,
her heart skipped. Then it started again, and
beat so fast and hard she was afraid he could
hear.

"Haley," he whispered. "I've wanted to do
this for a long time. Since that day you were
painting the mural at ROOTS."

What was he talking about? That day she
looked like something the cat yakked up? So
what—

And then his mouth took hers and she
couldn't think at all. The world stopped and

inside her it was like the Fourth of July—
bottle rockets going off. The flash, bang and
colors of fireworks and sparklers sparkling.

His lips moved softly, nibbling hers as his
arm encircled her waist and pulled her more
securely against him. She froze. What do I do
with my hands? she thought. She wanted to
feel his chest, put her arms around his neck.
The sensation of her breasts crushed against
him was amazing and stole the breath from
her lungs. All she could think about was getting closer, as near as possible to the hard
lines of his muscular body.

He took control, tipped his head to the side,
making the fit of their mouths more firm,
more perfect. The sparks he was creating
short-circuited her nerve endings and sent
sharp thrills of excitement pulsing through
every part of her. She could have stayed like
this forever.

Then he traced her lips with his tongue and
uncertainty fueled the panic waiting in the
wings. She wasn't sure what he wanted her
to do. She had no experience with a man like
him and he would know that if she didn't put
a stop to this. She couldn't bear it if he made
fun of her. Or worse, pitied her.

She put a palm on his chest and felt the tingle as part of her longed to explore the wide contours. But she couldn't risk it. He'd know her secret and she'd be humiliated. Putting pressure into the touch, she pushed him away, then backed out of the circle of his arms and started walking.

"Haley?" He caught up with her outside The Hitching Post. "Is something wrong?"

"No."

"Should I not have kissed you?" He dragged his fingers through his hair.

"Whatever."

"You're mad," he guessed.

She couldn't make herself meet his gaze. "Should I be?"

"You tell me."

Tell him what? He was the first guy who'd kissed her in years? Should she explain that the last one was in college and he'd barely progressed to kissing her good-night before she'd had to leave? Or maybe she could say that her world and her dreams shattered when she got the call that her mom was dead and any sort of personal life was put on hold indefinitely? Now too much time had passed and her social learning curve had been stunted?

Any man would have a reasonable expectation of experience from a twenty-four-year-old woman, but she was the exception to that rule. And it was too humiliating to explain, especially to Marlon Cates, that she was a social freak.

He'd been written up in People magazine. He'd dated actresses and models. Haley just knew she couldn't compete.

"Haley? Talk to me." He stopped at the door to the bar and grill and blocked it with his big body.

Without answering, she edged around him and inside the bar, where she knew what she was doing. Sort of. "Let's find a table."

It wasn't crowded on a weeknight and she grabbed menus from the hostess stand before choosing a booth not far from the door. A private table in the back wasn't on tonight's menu.

"Tuesday's special is pot roast," she said, working hard at looking over the food choices when the words wouldn't come into focus. It helped that she knew the menu by heart.

"Look," he said, "About what happened—"

"Hi." Erin Castro appeared beside them and smiled. "You two just can't stay away from this place."

Haley appreciated perkiness as much as

anyone, but not at the moment. "I'd like an iced tea and tonight's special. Can you put a rush on that? I need to get back to ROOTS."

"Make it two." Marlon handed over his menu without looking at the waitress. His gaze never left Haley's face. When they were alone, he continued. "Obviously you didn't want me to kiss you."

He couldn't be more wrong. She'd wanted it more than anything. This was one time she wished she hadn't gotten what she'd wanted because now it was so messed up.

"Forget it," she said.

"I think we should talk about what happened."

"Okay." But only because he wouldn't let it drop until she did. "I'm involved with the teen program and you're busy with your business." She forced herself to look at him and shrug. "The timing isn't right."

"You're hiding, Haley. You're burying your head in the sand."

"I don't know what you're talking about."

"Lying again. But let's leave that for now." His expression turned wry. "You know, when you bury your head in the sand it leaves your backside exposed."

"I'm not doing that. It's called being realistic." Before he could back her farther into the corner, Erin showed up with their meals.

"Let me know if you need anything else," she said, before slipping discreetly away.

Haley managed to dodge further talk about what happened but that didn't make the next thirty minutes any more comfortable. It was pretty awful. She brought up everything from weather to Thunder Canyon politics and Marlon asked her for some sketches of purses for a signature line at MC/TC. She couldn't remember ever being more miserable in her life and just played with her food until mercifully the plates were removed.

When Erin moved toward them, she knew a pitch for dessert was coming. Haley was better prepared for that than she'd been for Marlon's kiss.

"No dessert for me," she said to the other girl. "Can we just have the check?"

"Sure thing," the pretty blonde answered, pulling the receipt from her pocket.

"I'd like to split it," Haley said.

"No. I'm buying," Marlon protested.

"I pay for myself." Her tone was adamant.

With a puzzled frown, Erin looked from one to the other. "I'll just go get some experience doing separate checks while you two discuss this amongst yourselves."

When she was gone, Marlon said, "I insist on paying for your dinner. Tonight was my idea."

Not one of his better ones. Haley was sure he'd agree. This god-awful experience should take care of any possibility that he'd risk investing in her—either personally or professionally.

"Doesn't matter who suggested it. I want to pay for myself." She pulled out her wallet and put a twenty on the table. "Tell Erin to keep the change."

She slid out of the booth and left, listening for the sound of his footsteps behind her. When she didn't hear anything, she was both disappointed and relieved. The definition of conflict. The story of her life. She'd found out firsthand what harm socializing with Marlon could do.

Tonight she'd also found out she cared deeply what he thought of her. If she didn't, she'd have wise-cracked her way out of the awkwardness. Instead she froze. That was irrefutable evidence that the major crush she'd had on Marlon Cates years ago was not dead. That hadn't changed.

But she had. She was older, smarter, and knew better than to wait and hope for something more from him. If there was any silver lining in this fiasco, it was that her feelings were out in the open. She could protect herself. Maybe she was burying her head in the sand but that was the best way to circle the wagons and guard her heart.

As always she'd taken care of herself, had paid her own way. But she hoped that didn't mean paying a personal price for seeing Marlon outside of work. It could be very costly.

She would not let him hurt her again.

Chapter Eight

Haley stood by the bar at The Hitching Post and blew out a long breath. Of all the days to have a busier than usual lunch crowd, why did it have to be the day after she'd hardly slept? Of course, she'd hardly slept because of the loop in her head that continuously flashed images of the disastrous dinner with Marlon.

From breathtaking kiss to dinner check, it was hard to count the ways she'd made a fool of herself. He was probably counting his lucky stars that his community service was almost half over. Or he was looking for another way to ~~repay his~~ debt to society so that he never had to see her again. Well, she was on board with that because then she wouldn't have to see him, either. On top of that, she never wanted to hear his name again for as long as she lived.

Erin Castro plopped down on the bar stool beside her and heaved a tired sigh. "Is it always that busy?"

"No." Haley levered herself onto the other high chair.

"Good."

"I noticed a lot of moms with kids," Haley said. "My guess is that they're shopping for back-to-school stuff and topping off the outing with lunch. A last hurrah to the summer."

"Again I say good." Erin put an elbow on the bar and rested her cheek in her palm. "I'm getting too old for this."

Haley laughed. "You're what? Twenty-one?"

"Twenty-five." The blonde grinned. "But thanks. And you didn't have to be so charitable after the generous tip you left me last night."

It was a testament to willpower that Haley managed to hold in a wince. Apparently it was too much to hope that the other woman hadn't noticed the tension. Brush it off, she thought.

"Waitresses are the best tippers," she said.

"You were already gone, so you couldn't know, but Marlon's tip was better."

"He can afford it." Haley had meant the words to be casual, teasing, light, but the delivery had a snap to it.

"Word on the street is that he's a high-powered businessman. A millionaire. And my own experience is that he gives good gratuity. I wonder if he ever worked in the food service industry," Erin mused.

"So you made pretty good money last night." Change the subject, Haley thought. No Marlon talk. "You're doing a great job for having been here such a short time, Erin. If you can handle a crowd like we just had, you'll be fine."

"Thanks. Coming from you that's a real compliment. So how long have you worked here at The Hitching Post?"

It felt like forever. And when ungrateful thoughts like that crept in, she reminded herself that she was lucky to have the job. Lucky the manager of the bar and grill had taken a chance on a desperate eighteen-year-old without skills who badly needed a way to take care of her family. But there were times when she wished for more. And Marlon's reaction to her sketches had resurrected the dream. For all the good dreaming did.

"I've worked here going on six years now," Haley answered.

"Wow. That's a long time." Erin's blue eyes sparked with interest. "You probably know a lot about the people in Thunder Canyon. Working in a place like this."

"I'm not sure I follow." Haley stared at the other woman.

"It's just that everyone in town comes in here. Dinner. Drinks. They talk." She shrugged. "You're bound to hear things."

Haley did hear things. She got information about the folks in Thunder Canyon, but gossiping seemed wrong. Taken out of context or repeated from person to person, details got fuzzy until nothing about the original story was the truth. Was Erin a gossip? Or simply wanting to bond with her over Thunder Canyon?

"I talk to a lot of people every day," she hedged.

"I'm a newbie." Erin laughed and there was a tinge of self-consciousness. "But you already know that. And I'm trying to get to know everyone."

"It's a small town. That's not hard." Haley could understand that she was trying to fit in.

"Not if you grew up here." Erin looked eager. "I'm trying to put names and faces together. Let's take Marlon. There's another guy who comes in. Looks just like him—"

"Matthew Cates—Marlon's twin."

"Which would explain why they look alike. Don't they have another brother?"

"Two, actually," Haley answered. "Marshall and Mitchell are both older. The twins are the youngest of the Cates boys."

"Don't they have a lot of cousins?" Erin asked, a little too casually. It looked forced.

"You might be thinking about the Traubs. D.J. and Dax. But they're brothers. No relation to the Cates family. Just longtime friends."

Erin's forehead puckered in concentration. "What about Bo Clifton? The guy who's running for Mayor?"

"You heard about that?"

"It's all over town," Erin confirmed. "Doesn't he have cousins?"

Haley tapped her lip as she thought. "Grant Clifton. He's the manager at Thunder Canyon Resort."

"It seems like I heard he has a sister?"

"Elise. She's my best friend," Haley confirmed. And how she missed her friend these days. She'd give anything to have someone to talk to about Marlon. Maybe talking would help to get him off her mind. Sounded like the theme of a country western tune. "But she lives in Billings now."

Erin nodded thoughtfully, then said, "So how long has Marlon been your boyfriend?"

"He's not."

"Really?" The other waitress tucked her blond hair behind her ear. "I thought you guys had hooked up. After last night…"

Haley squirmed. Erin's social cues and interpersonal observations were really out of whack if she thought last night's events were about a relationship. "What makes you think he's my boyfriend? Based on what you saw?"

"You mean because you were fighting?" Erin waved her hand dismissively. "A lovers' quarrel."

Way off the mark—and not very likely now. Haley had acted like he had the plague because she had no idea how to kiss him back. He would never risk a repeat and that was too bad. Because she could definitely see how a kiss—especially from Marlon—could be life-altering. Ever since last night's close encounter of the personal kind, her hormones had been giving her a hard time. There was a knot in the pit of her stomach that felt like frustration on crack.

And she didn't know how to make it go away.

Since Marlon didn't plan to stay in Thunder Canyon, it was probably for the best that she got a failing grade in Kissing 101. A repeat of the experience would not help her stay aloof. Which she needed to do if she planned on not getting attached to him.

"We're not lovers," Haley finally said. "In fact, I'm not sure we're even friends."

"Really? He seemed pretty upset. So did you, for that matter. If there's nothing between you, there'd be no reason for that."

He was upset when she left? That information sent a small shimmy of pleasure through her. But hope was a place she couldn't afford to go.

"Trust me, there's nothing between Marlon and me."

"Too bad. He's really cute. And he's got a lot of money?" Erin looked like she was working very hard at appearing barely interested. But there was an underlying intensity to her questions that made Haley wary.

She was about to say they should get back

to work and end this conversation when an older couple came into the restaurant and were seated in Erin's section.

"Gotta go." She'd noticed, too. "We should get together for a drink some evening."

"Maybe." Haley wasn't ready to commit. She was almost sure that something was up with Erin and didn't want to jump into a friendship based on hidden agendas. "I'm pretty busy with ROOTS right now."

"The teen mentor program." Over her shoulder Erin said, "Let me know if I can help."

Haley watched her smile at the customers and wondered about her over-enthusiastic interest in Marlon. Jealousy reared its ugly head again. It was one of her less attractive qualities, but acknowledging it was half the battle in suppressing the tendency. At least she hoped so.

Since Marlon had come back to Thunder Canyon, she seemed to be acknowledging and suppressing a lot where he was concerned— both her attraction to him and the crush that refused to die.

She sighed and shook her head as she slid down from her bar stool, muttering to herself. "This whole suppression thing needs work. A lot of work."

* * *

Marlon sat beside Roy in the folding chairs that faced the corner TV at ROOTS. They were playing a video game and he was getting his ass kicked because his head was on what happened between him and Haley last night.

When the door behind them opened, he knew right away it wasn't a group of kids. They were usually so noisy it would be impossible to sneak up on a glass of water. Even outside on the sidewalk you could hear talking, teasing, laughing. And if girls were there, the decibel level went up loud enough to shatter glass in the next county.

The person who'd just come in was too quiet and suddenly it felt as if the temperature in the room dropped to sub-zero. Plus the smell of her perfume made his blood hum, his skin burn.

Haley.

He couldn't wait to see her and dreaded it at the same time. That was just whacked for a decisive guy like himself. Somehow he'd ticked her off when he'd kissed her last night and he didn't have a clue what he'd done wrong. It wasn't as if that was his first time kissing a girl. He'd had a lot of experience. Tons. He knew what he was doing and all the signs said Haley had been into it. She'd been breathing just as hard as he was; she'd made that turned-on, breathy little sound that drove him completely nuts.

Then all of a sudden she had pushed him away and treated him like an ax murderer. What was up with that?

Haley walked into the storage room leaving the scent of her drifting behind him. His skin felt too tight and another, stronger flash of heat rolled through him.

"Hi, Roy," she called out.

"Hey." The kid glanced sideways, game forgotten. "That was weird."

Marlon set his control on the floor. "What?"

"She didn't say hi to you."

"I noticed." There was a lot she wasn't saying to him. Volumes. And there were no signs that would be changing anytime soon. He'd sure like to be a mind reader right about now.

"What did you do?"

Since Marlon didn't think it was appropriate to discuss kissing her, he said, "Nothing."

Roy looked at him. "Must be somethin', dude. She's glacial."

"Yeah, well, if global warming can melt the polar ice pack maybe it will work on her, too."

Marlon stood. "You've got supervision now. I've been relieved of duty. I'll see you later."

"You're bailing on me?" Roy complained.

Marlon looked down. "Are you going to tell me where you live?"

The teenage mask of intensity slipped into place. "No way."

"Then I'm bailing on you."

Without another word, Marlon walked outside and started down the wooden sidewalk. He was halfway to The Hitching Post when he heard a horn honk behind him. Turning, he recognized the Cates Construction truck as it pulled over and stopped beside him.

His twin, Matt, was behind the wheel. "Hey, bro."

Marlon leaned his forearms on the passenger-side window frame. "What's up?"

"I'm on my way back to a job. We're doing the foundation for Connor McFarlane's house."

"Need some help?" Marlon could sure use some physical work to get rid of the restless energy that made him want to put his fist through a wall.

His brother studied him for several moments before saying, "Hop in."

Marlon remembered Haley asking him if

it was like looking in a mirror when he was with his brother. Their faces were practically identical, as was their dark hair and eyes. But they were different in a lot of ways. Matt was more muscular, a side effect of physical labor, working with his hands. He was also more serious, some said somber. According to their mother, he was just more mature. And loyal to a fault. Haley would never tell Matt that commitment wasn't his strength.

"That's a pretty fierce look on your face," his brother observed.

Marlon met his gaze for a moment. "I've got a lot on my mind."

"Want to talk about it?"

"No."

What was there to say? Haley was mad. He had no idea why. But he was only there to do his community service, so what did it matter whether or not she liked him? Except the hell of it was that it did matter and he wanted it to stop mattering.

Matt knew him well enough to leave him to his thoughts and they were quiet until they got to the construction site. And it was a beaut, Marlon thought when the truck pulled into the clearing. Connor McFarlane had picked a nice piece of land outside of town. A few trees had been cleared, but the majority were saved. The way the earth was dug out for the foundation showed him the general layout of the house, giving the front a spectacular view of the mountains, the best possible view as a matter of fact. Matt would have spent a lot of time getting the orientation just right for maximum panorama potential. His brother was incredibly good at his job.

He opened the driver's-side door and jumped out of the truck, then reached in for his tool belt and buckled it on. Marlon followed him over the uneven ground to a stack of lumber.

"This is going to be a great house," he said.

"Big." Matt studied the ground and nodded with satisfaction. "It will be good for the Cates Construction portfolio."

"Where's the rest of your crew?"

His brother grabbed a piece of wood. "They're done for the day. Can't afford to pay overtime, but there's still a couple more hours of daylight and I don't want to waste it." He looked up and suddenly grinned. "And I found some free labor."

"It'll cost you," Marlon warned. "You won't know when or how much, but it will."

"I'm scared." Matt positioned the board

where he wanted it and fitted another in. "We're pouring the foundation soon and it needs to be framed first."

"Yeah. I figured," Marlon said wryly. "I lift a hammer from time to time—when I have the time. It hasn't been that long since I worked for Cates Construction."

"You're a pansy," Matt joked. "Soft and sweet with your cushy job behind your desk in L.A."

"Never judge a man until you walk a mile in his shoes." Marlon smiled.

Unlike dealing with the mercurial Haley Anderson, this back and forth with his brother was familiar. The house foundation wasn't there but the same couldn't be said of the one he had with Matt. It felt good. And the truth was they hadn't worked like this for a while. Or talked.

"So what's new?"

Matt glanced up. "I guess you haven't heard."

"What?"

"Dillon Traub is going to take over for Marshall as the on-site sports doctor at Thunder Canyon Resort."

Dillon was Dax and D.J. Traub's cousin. Through them, Marlon had met him and liked him a lot. He was fun, casual and confident without being obnoxious. Then a thought hit him.

"Why is he filling in? Where's Marshall going?"

Matt slid him a pitying look that said he really needed to stay in the loop. "Marshall and Mia, that's his wife in case you haven't heard—"

"I know he's married. And I've actually met Mia. She's great. What I didn't know is that they're going somewhere."

"In September he's taking her on an extended working vacation," Matt explained.

"Working how?"

"Mia has finished nursing school and they'll be doing some sightseeing as well as visiting counseling centers that she hopes to model her own after."

"I didn't know that," Marlon said.

His twin nodded. "She's using her inheritance to start a grief counseling center for women."

Marlon thought about Haley, the overwhelming anguish she must have experienced after her mom died. "Sounds like a really worthwhile undertaking. The Anderson family could have used something like that."

Matt swiped his forearm over his sweaty forehead as he nodded. "Yeah. I don't know how Haley did what she did. Raising Angie and Austin at the same time she was dealing with her mother's loss…and she did a great job of it."

"Yeah." Haley was a hell of a woman, Marlon thought. As was his sister-in-law. "Good for Mia. I hope the two of them have a great trip. And I can't think of anyone better than Dillon to fill in for Marshall."

Too bad he wouldn't be around when the other man took over for his brother. Moving around a lot was the downside of doing what Marlon did. And that meant missing out on a lot of stuff. It never used to bother him, but now? Discontent was the best description he could come up with.

Marlon watched his brother fit more wood together and nail it in place. "You know, it's a good thing Dillon is rich and the heir to Traub Oil Industries."

"I'm sure Dillon wouldn't argue with you on that point." Matt looked up, a wry expression on his face. "But why do you think so?"

"Because he's not locked into a nine-to-five job and can pick and choose where and when to practice medicine."

Matt rested his forearm on his thigh. "Now that I think about it, he always knew he wanted to be a doctor when he grew up."

"Don't sound so envious." Marlon handed his brother another two-by-four. "You always liked building stuff. From Tinkertoys to Erector sets, you'd make things. I envied that."

"You think I've always been sure of myself?" Matt asked.

"Duh," Marlon answered.

"Not so much. Have you forgotten that I'm a law school dropout?"

"Only because it was never really your dream," Marlon defended. "Mom and Dad wanted you to be a lawyer."

"That's not an excuse," Matt retorted.

"I'm not saying it was. Just that kids try to please their parents."

Marlon thought of Roy and wondered if he'd run from parental pressure to do or be something he didn't want. Then he thought about Haley, who hadn't had the guidance of parents nearly as long as she should have. And now she was trying to help other kids who needed a steadying hand. Again he realized that she was a very special woman.

"In the long run, life is all about finding something you love to do," Marlon said. "And you like working with your hands. It's what you're good at. Construction is a no-brainer for you."

"Like you're good at business."

"Yeah. But it fries my ass that you're good at business, too." Marlon grinned when his twin made a scoffing sound. "Really. It's not fair that you can do both equally as well. And you really love it."

Matt looked up. "How do you feel about what you're doing?"

"You mean my company?"

"No, the community service. The need for speed brought you down, bro. How's it going at ROOTS?"

"It's living up to its name," he said ruefully. "I'm planted in one spot. At least until the end of August."

"You might be stuck in one spot, but at least the scenery is good. Haley is hot. You could be stuck working for a crabby ninety-year-old with a gray bun in her hair and a stick up her butt."

No argument there, Marlon thought. Haley was pretty as a picture and twice as sweet. Until last night. "She's not ninety and I've never seen her hair in a bun."

"So what's wrong?"

"Nothing."

Matt's expression was scornful. "This is me, Mar. I know you better than anyone."

"You don't know everything."

"Then tell me."

Marlon met his brother's gaze. "I was engaged in college and she took me for a bundle of money."

"I hate it when you're right." Matt stared at him. "I didn't know that."

"She played the purity card. Said she didn't believe in sleeping together before marriage. So I proposed and wanted to set a date."

"Don't tell me. She was in no hurry to do that."

"Right in one," Marlon said ruefully. "She claimed she had a lot of debt from her father's medical problems and didn't want to burden me with it."

"So you wrote her a check," Matt guessed.

"With too many zeroes. After which she disappeared." He hated being made a fool of. "It's not something I look back on with pride."

"I can understand that. But don't let that put you off women altogether."

"Who says I'm doing that?" Marlon asked, suddenly defensive.

"Something's going on. What's up?"

He knew there was no point in putting his twin off. Matt knew him too well and wouldn't let up until he had the information he wanted. "Haley. All grown up, I mean."

Matt stood and rested his hands on his hips. "You're hung up on her. And running scared because of the girl who ripped you off."

Marlon waved his hand dismissively. "What have you been smoking?"

"There it is again," his brother said, pointing. "Defensive. Another sign that something's different with you this time."

"You're crazy."

"No, you are. You need to embrace it, bro. She could be 'the one.'"

"The one?"

"To finally tame my restless twin," Matt explained.

"No way." Marlon shook his head. "Just call me the happy wanderer."

"The more they protest, the harder they fall," Matt teased.

Marlon didn't like the turn of this conversation and it was time to put it out of its misery. "Even if I was interested in Haley, and that's a big if, I'm not the settling down sort."

"Where have I heard that before?" Matt snapped his fingers. "Oh, yeah. Big brother

Marshall said it right before he met Mia. Maybe even after they met. He swore up and down he wasn't the kind of man who did relationships. He was just like you, carefree and commitment-phobic."

"And your point is?"

"He's married and getting ready to go on his honeymoon. I've never seen him happier."

"Again I ask, what's your point?" Marlon knew he'd be sorry for asking, but the words were out before he could stop them.

An unfortunate byproduct of verbal sparring with his brother was getting backed into a corner. Fighting his way out didn't always make his comebacks very smart.

"Just saying. Haley could be the one." Matt smiled. "Never say never."

There was no way to win this argument so Marlon didn't try. No matter how much he'd liked kissing Haley, how much he liked the lady herself, clearly the feeling wasn't mutual. Although he would swear the attraction was. But could he trust it? Was pushing him away some kind of game with her?

There was no point in sorting out the questions. The bigger problem was finding a way to shut down his festering feelings, because he had two more weeks of community service left. That was more than enough time for a lot to happen.

And he didn't want anything to happen. Not with Haley. He would rather walk barefoot over broken glass than do anything else to hurt her.

Chapter Nine

"Guys don't make cookies."

Haley looked up as Roy stirred chocolate chips into the second batch of thick dough. They were in her small, cozy kitchen working on the old oak table. The six chairs were against the wall where inspirational sayings were hung beside her mother's copper pots and decorative plates. With walls painted a soft yellow, the white cotton curtains at the window pulled everything together as they overlooked the front yard.

Thank goodness she'd been able to hang on to this place after her mother died. Not only for Austin and Angie's sake, but for her own, as well. She still felt her mother's presence and wondered what her response would have been if Austin griped about baking like Roy just did.

"Is there a rule somewhere that says guys can't make cookies?" she asked.

He looked up from his job. "It's chick work."

"Has anyone ever mentioned to you that whining is marginally tolerable in a two-year-old, but incredibly unattractive not to mention annoying in a teenager?"

"Just saying." Roy grinned. "If any of my friends saw me with a wooden spoon and a bowl of dough, I'd never live it down."

"Do your friends live close by? Is there a chance they could see what you're doing?"

"Did you think I wouldn't notice that?"

"I wasn't subtle?" she asked innocently.

"Not even a little bit." He grinned again. "Nice try."

"Okay then. Back to cookies. You might be surprised how many men know their way around a kitchen. Some of the top chefs in the world are men."

She studied him, his blue eyes unreadable, light brown hair shaggy around his lean face. Definitely a hottie as the teen girls had mentioned more than once. Yesterday he'd said longingly how good home-baked cookies tasted and she realized how long it had been since she'd baked them. This was a rare day off, giving her time to do just that. Angie and Austin had left for work at the resort a while ago and she'd nudged Roy into helping her. A dollop of guilt had been judiciously applied in the nudging process. Apparently he needed another dose.

The muscles in his biceps bunched as he wielded the wooden spoon, grunting from the effort. "I hate baking."

"Me, too." She met his surprised gaze. "What? Just because I'm a girl I have to like it?"

"I didn't say anything."

"It's written all over your face." She lifted one shoulder in a shrug. "There's my shocking secret. I hate cooking."

He stood the spoon up straight in the thick mixture. "Then why are you doing it?"

"You said the kids like homemade better than store-bought cookies."

"So? They can survive without 'em. Everyone has to live with disappointment."

She happened to be looking at him when he made the comment. Was he quoting someone who'd said it to him? Was he running from some form of disappointment? Sooner or later this had to be sorted out because the situation couldn't go on much longer. The call to his mother had been a while ago and all the poor woman knew was that he'd been alive then.

If she and Marlon couldn't get Roy to open up pretty soon, they'd have to involve the authorities. It wasn't her first choice because she wanted the kids to feel they could trust her with anything. But talking through problems was the first step in facing them. Roy was simply hiding.

"Yeah," she finally said. "Everyone does have to live with disappointment. But not when it comes to chocolate chip cookies. They've been known to make stronger men than you sing like a canary."

"Not me." He glanced at a grouping of pictures on the wall behind her.

There was one about parenthood and a saying that children learned what they lived. Another of a cow because her mother had liked cows. And a cross-stitch of a breadbasket. Her favorite was the embroidery that her mom had made. Just words on a linen square. "There are but two lasting bequests we can give our children—roots and wings."

Haley glanced at it, then said, "My mother

made that. She said it means that kids should always know where they come from, where home is. Where they're loved. But a parent should also infuse their children with the courage to strike out and find their own destiny. Never be afraid to follow a dream knowing you can go home again. It's where the name of the mentoring program came from."

"ROOTS," he said.

She nodded. "It's my dream. To help kids, like the people here in Thunder Canyon helped me when my mom died."

"I get it," he said.

"Good." Hoping he would say more about where he came from, she waited, but he just looked thoughtful. It wasn't quite time to push yet. Sighing, she indicated a pan full of cooled cookies beside the stove. "Why don't you put those in that plastic container."

"Okay." He lifted a spatula from a crockery jar on the counter and went to work. "So, speaking of ROOTS—"

Something in his voice made her look up. A hint of vulnerability that maybe he'd tell her more about himself. "Yes?"

"What's up with you and Marlon?"

Hearing the name of the man she kept trying to put out of her mind was unexpected and she missed the cookie sheet when she scraped dough off her spoon. It plopped on the distressed wood floor. No way this floor could be as distressed as her, she thought. Talking about the man who'd kissed her wasn't her idea of a good time. Odd, now that she thought about it. There was a time she'd dreamed about kissing Marlon and it finally happened, in front of ROOTS, the dream that she'd made happen. She was one for one on the dream front. One was going well, the other? Not so much.

"There's nothing up with me and Marlon." Turning her back, she grabbed a paper towel, then stooped to clean up the mess. It was a good way to hide the reaction she couldn't conceal. Kids didn't miss much.

But Roy was persistent. "Then why didn't you say hello to him yesterday?"

"What? Where?" She threw the gooey paper in the trash, then picked up the two teaspoons and resumed dropping dough on the cookie sheet.

"You came in to ROOTS after work and said hi to me but not to Marlon. You always say hello to everyone. What's up with that?"

"Really? I didn't realize." She brushed a knuckle on her cheek and remembered what

Marlon had said about lying. Was her nose growing? "I'm sure it wasn't a big deal."

"Was, too. He bailed right after that. It was tense. And don't tell me it's just my imagination. Or I don't know what tension is, because I do. He was tense and so were you."

"It's nothing you need to worry about. The fact is, his community service will be over soon. He'll be leaving town."

Her attempt to sound upbeat was a dismal failure. Even she heard the sadness in her voice. Something about saying those words out loud made her chest squeeze so tight it was a challenge to draw in a breath of air. So much for the unspoken lie that his kiss didn't change anything.

"I think you really like him," Roy stated firmly.

Keep it light, she thought. Uncomplicated. And as truthful as possible. "Of course I like him. I like everyone. You shouldn't read anything into it."

"I wish you'd stop treating me like a kid."

"Why would you think I am?" she asked.

"I've got eyes. I've been around. I know stuff. I'm almost eighteen. A man."

Haley rested her spoons on the lip of the big bowl as she looked at him. "Reaching a milestone age doesn't automatically mean you're a man, or a woman either, for that matter. It's what you do day in and day out that makes you an adult."

He put the lid on the big plastic container. "You mean like what you did? Stepping up for Angie and Austin after your mom died?"

"That's right."

"What about your dad?" he asked. "Was he dead, too?"

To her he was. His leaving had broken Nell Anderson's heart. Haley remembered being a little girl and asking her mom about him. The soul-deep sadness in her eyes when Nell had answered that he just didn't love them enough to stay. He'd already been gone a long time, but her mother was still sad and lonely. The child Haley had been wished she and her brother and sister were enough for their mom, but the sadness never went away.

And Haley never resented the man who'd fathered her more than when he wasn't there for his kids after losing their mother. It had been six years, but anger still made her voice shake and her hands tremble when she talked about him. The feelings were real and raw and maybe Roy should know he wasn't the only person on the face of the planet with problems. He needed to see, so she turned off her own emotional sensors and let her feelings show.

"My father was never a man," she said angrily. "Real men don't walk out on a wife and three children who need him."

The hostile tone got Roy's attention. "Do you remember him?"

"No." It was on the tip of her tongue to say she was glad, but that was childish. Running away. "It makes me sad and angry. I try to tell myself that he's the one who missed out, but the truth is Angie, Austin and I all lost out on something because we didn't know our father. He disappeared and avoided his responsibilities."

Thoughtfully, Roy leaned back against the Formica countertop. "So you do think I'm a kid."

"It doesn't matter what I think. Only you can decide whether or not you're running away from something."

"Marlon isn't running," he said out of the blue.

It was official. Marlon Cates was a favorite of everyone. Women wanted to be with him and guys wanted to be his friend. She was the only one who fell into some gray area of pretending he didn't do a thing for her.

"I'm not sure what you mean," she said.

"Community service. He's here and doing what he has to do. He's not running out on his punishment. He's sticking around. That makes him a man."

Wow, was he a man, she thought as memories of their kiss popped into her head. Roy blinked at her and, for just a second, she was afraid she'd said the words out loud. Then his expression turned pensive, making him look like the confused teenager she was trying to help.

"He's taking the consequences for his actions. Like a man. I can't argue with that."

Roy suddenly grinned. "And I still say you like him."

She couldn't argue with that either, much as she wished she could. She'd like to believe that Roy was just a kid who didn't really understand grown-up relationships. It was a fact that Marlon was doing the responsible thing and making a difference. The teens looked up to him. That was all good.

It was her liking him that was bad.

Unlike how her father had walked out, Marlon's leaving wasn't going to be a surprise. She had fair warning. There was time to prepare. And yet she didn't know how to stop the runaway, out-of-control freight train her feelings had become. Every indication was that they couldn't be stopped. She'd tried, but even this teenager had seen through her.

Since she couldn't seem to get a handle on what was simmering between them, maybe Marlon could stop it. Who could blame him after the way she'd acted. Even Roy had noticed. From now on she expected Marlon to be just as cool toward her, maybe put the brakes on her feelings.

She had to keep trying. There was a time limit on how long Marlon was sticking around, but heartbreak had no shelf life. It could last forever.

She could be THE ONE.

Ever since yesterday, when his twin had said that about Haley, the words had been capitalized in Marlon's mind and wouldn't leave him alone. He'd come for breakfast at The Hitching Post and so far was just having coffee, wishing it wasn't too early for something stronger. He was still brooding about Matt comparing him to their older brother

Marshall, who'd sworn that he wasn't the marrying kind.

For the record, Marlon's situation was completely different. He didn't live in Thunder Canyon. He had a life in Los Angeles and Haley hadn't bothered to hide her opinion of the place. Plus she'd made no secret of the fact that she didn't respect him much. Even Roy had noticed the cold shoulder.

How could she be "the one"? In order to tame the restless Cates twin, she needed to show some interest. If she was interested, she had a funny way of showing it.

"You're in my seat."

The deep voice and hostile tone made Marlon look up. Ben Walters was looming over him, a walking, talking crabby sign that this day could actually get worse. The two of them had never gotten along and Marlon wasn't in the mood to play nice now.

"I don't see your name on it," Marlon said.

"If you were around more, you'd know they call this Ben's booth." The other man pointed to the erotic picture of Lily Divine over the bar. "Old guy like me knows the best seat in the house when he sees it."

Marlon studied the portrait of the scantily clad woman. It had nothing to do with why he'd sat here, but now that the benefits had been brought to his attention, he grinned. "Old has nothing to do with it."

The man's mouth twitched, as if he were fighting a smile. "Still, this is my usual place."

"Maybe we could share it." The fact that this geezer was a close friend of Haley's wasn't his primary motivation, but it wasn't exactly a deal breaker either.

Ben looked thoughtful for several moments, then nodded. "On one condition."

"Name it."

"You sit on the other side of the booth."

"Done." Marlon slid his coffee mug across the table, then got up and sat with his back to Lily Divine.

Ben had just settled on the seat when Hitching Post manager Linda Powell brought over two menus and a steaming mug of black coffee. The pretty brunette put it down in front of the older man and smiled.

"This is a first." She glanced at the two of them and one of her dark eyebrows lifted questioningly. "Has there been a shift in the universe and no one told me?"

"Some things Marlon and me see eye to

eye on." Ben slid a look at the portrait and a corner of his mouth lifted.

"Are you ready to order or do you need a minute?" She was talking to Marlon. "It seems like you should know that menu by heart. You're going to give Ben some competition as our best customer."

"The food is good." Marlon shrugged and without any waitress prompting said, "I'll have the special. Eggs over medium. Hash browns. Sausage. And a side of pancakes with maple syrup."

"Make it two."

"I thought you were watching your cholesterol." Linda stared at the other man over the half glasses sitting on the end of her nose.

"Here's the thing." Ben handed her the menu. "I quit smoking. Gave up beer for a glass of red wine now and then. And never touch a salt shaker. Every once in a while a man's gotta get wild."

"With sausage and eggs?" Marlon's mouth curved up. "Are you sure the excitement won't be too much for you?"

"Smart aleck." Ben pointed a finger at him, but a twinkle lurked in his light blue eyes. "You should learn to respect your elders, son."

Marlon met his gaze—man to man. "I have a great deal of respect for you."

"I'll have these orders up in a jiffy." The brunette flashed another flirty smile at Ben before taking both menus and moving away.

Marlon watched the older man stare appreciatively at the sway of her hips as she walked and wondered if the widower was involved with the waitress. If so, he was happy for them.

He couldn't resist saying, "She's sweet on you."

"Yeah."

"There's no accounting for taste," Marlon teased.

"Can't argue with that."

A shrewdness slid into those wise eyes and Marlon had a feeling they were no longer talking about Ben and Linda. But if he meant Haley was sweet on Marlon, he was wrong. Her taste didn't run to businessmen from Los Angeles. That thought made him wonder… How did her taste in men run?

Maybe she was dating someone and thought Ben knew about it. Because in a small town, people always knew that kind of stuff.

He took a sip of cold coffee and said as casually as possible. "You and Haley are pretty close."

"That we are." Ben nodded once. "She's like the daughter I never had."

"Then you'd probably know if she's seeing someone."

"Sees lots of people. Goes with the territory when you work in a place like this."

"That's not what I meant. Is she—"

"I know what you meant. Wasn't born yesterday, which we've already established."

Marlon sighed. "You're not making this easy."

"Good." The older man nodded with satisfaction.

"Is there a guy?" Marlon held up his hand before a witty comeback came in his direction. "I mean is there someone she goes out with on a regular basis?"

The idea of her with another guy tied his gut in knots and made his chest feel like an elephant plopped his backside down right smack in the center of it. Haley dating someone else felt wrong on every level.

Ben thought about the question for several moments then simply said, "Nope."

Linda picked that moment to come back carrying a tray loaded with food. She set plates of steaming potatoes, eggs and pancakes in front of them. Marlon had been starving when he sat down, but had lost his appetite in the last couple of minutes.

"Nope, what?" Linda asked.

"Marlon wanted to know if Haley has a boyfriend."

As the two stared at him, Marlon was now fidgeting like a teenager meeting his girlfriend's parents for the first time. He could change the subject, but now that he'd popped open this can of worms, his squirmy curiosity refused to slither back inside.

Linda slid the empty plastic tray under her arm and looked at Ben. "I can't recall Haley going out with anyone. At least not around here. Can you?"

"Like I said... Nope."

"Not in Thunder Canyon. If she did we'd know."

That was pretty much what Marlon figured. But her behavior when he'd kissed her made him suspicious. Something was up. "What does that mean? Not here in Thunder Canyon?"

"She went away to college."

Marlon tried to remember if he'd known

that and couldn't. Now it seemed vitally important.

"It was just for a couple of months," Linda continued, her forehead creased as she thought back. "Then her mom was killed and she had to come back for Angie and Austin. Poor thing."

He knew that. What he wanted was current events in her life. He was impatient for information and tamped down the urge to hurry them up.

"Now that you mention it, wasn't there a guy at college that she talked about?" Ben pushed a pat of butter over the top of his pancakes and poured on syrup from the small glass container on the side of the plate.

A guy? In college?

"Were they...close?" Marlon asked, hearing the edge in his voice.

"Must have been if she mentioned him to you," Linda commented.

"But you never met the guy?" Marlon looked from one to the other, trying to figure out what all this meant.

Ben took a bite of egg and chewed thoughtfully. "I'd remember if he'd showed up. Never did. And believe me, that girl could've used another pair of shoulders to hold up all the crap going on."

Marlon's imagination went full throttle and filled in the blanks. She'd gone away to school and hooked up with someone. It was hot and heavy then tragedy brought her home. For good. But the guy wasn't there to support her during the worst time of her life. He'd disillusioned her. Broke her heart.

Marlon stabbed his fork into the stack of pancakes. "The bastard wasn't there when she needed him most. That would make it pretty hard for her to trust anyone."

"That'd be my guess." Ben nodded. "She tries to hide it, but there's a sadness in her eyes. Too much. She's been hurt pretty bad."

And she didn't want to take a chance again.

It made sense.

Then Marlon had to go and kiss her. Just like he'd done all those years ago. He'd kissed her at the football fundraiser. Just like that, quiet and timid Haley Anderson had really gotten his attention. He'd been surprised at the passion simmering beneath her shy surface and wanted to get to know her better. Asking her for a date had been the plan and she'd seemed eager for him to call.

But apparently Ben Walters had heard

about it. Gotta love the way things spread in a small town. It had ticked him off when Ben warned him away, told him not to mess with Haley. He'd wanted to tell the old meddler to mind his own business, then changed his mind and told Ben he wouldn't make trouble. That'd be a first, the old man had said.

Marlon met the older man's gaze and knew he was remembering it, too. "All those years ago... Staying away from Haley was the best thing to do. You were right about me."

Ben shook his head. "Nope."

"Excuse me?" Marlon had thought he'd agree and rub it in.

"Frank and Edie Cates are good parents. All you boys grew up to be fine men."

"I didn't think you liked me. I'm flattered."

"Don't be." Ben shifted his bulk on the bench seat. "Not trying to be your friend. Just honest. Word around town is you're taking responsibility for what you did wrong and actually helping those kids at ROOTS. Not to mention Haley. Just saying...I was wrong about you. You're a good man."

Try telling that to Haley, Marlon thought darkly. She'd been smart to push him away. He had a reputation with women. The kind he dated were into fun, games and publicity.

But Haley was different. Not so shy and timid anymore, but solid and sweet and sexy. She was an all or nothing kind of girl who had him thinking more about all while the nothing part looked less and less inviting.

Something about Haley pulled at him with a steady strength that was becoming increasingly difficult to ignore. But she'd had more bad stuff happen to her than most people did in a lifetime.

The last thing he would do was be one more thing on her bad list. While he was stuck in Thunder Canyon he had to find the willpower to leave her be before he had to leave for good.

Chapter Ten

It was getting late, almost time to close ROOTS up for the night. But the three teen-age girls, two flanking Haley on the sofa and one leaning over the back of it, were really into critically assessing her drawings in general, and handbag designs in particular.

In the corner of the room opposite the TV and video games, Roy and Austin were huddled around the donated computer on its donated desk. The girls had teased them about hiding in their "man cave."

Haley picked up a red pencil, made a few strokes and added a bow on the evening bag.

"This would look really nice in black satin. Maybe some sequins on the bow."

"Ooh," the girls all said together.

"I've never seen anything in the store as cute as that," said Becky Harmon, a hazel-eyed brunette new to ROOTS.

Kim and Jerilyn had brought her with them tonight. Haley had heard rumors about her older brother, a senior running back on the Thunder Canyon High School football team. Word on the street was that he'd been caught using performance-enhancing drugs to increase his chances of getting notice from college scouts and possibly a scholarship. Money was tight since their dad was out of work. That would mean even more trauma and tension at home.

It made Haley feel good that she'd provided somewhere the girl could go and forget about real-life problems for a while. She could laugh, be silly and talk about girly stuff.

On her sketch pad, Haley drew a small, slim bag with a shoulder strap and snap closure. Then she sketched a rear view of the same purse. "What do you think about a decorative zipper?"

"Awesome." Kim was leaning over the back of the sofa.

Jerilyn tapped her lip thoughtfully. "Maybe a sort of big, chunky one with fringe on the tab."

"Great idea." The scratchy sound of Haley's pencil was the only sound in the room as the teen audience watched her bring the idea to life on paper. "There. What do you think?"

"I want to buy one," Kim said, enthusiastically. "It's just the right size. Not too big. Not a murse."

"A what?" Haley glanced over her shoulder at the pretty blonde.

"You know. Murse. Mom purse."

No, she didn't know and the thought made her a little sad. That flash of pain at missing her mom only happened rarely now, but this was one of those times. Some of it was hearing the kids talk about their parents and remembering why this program was so important to her. She glanced over at Austin, who was pointing something out to Roy on the computer monitor. Her mom would be proud of this place and her three kids, who had turned a horrible loss into something positive.

The thought didn't take away her fear of going through more pain and darkness again. She had her family and would protect them with everything she had. But the remembered sadness made her more determined than ever not to let anyone else close.

The front door opened and Marlon Cates walked in, all loose-limbed dash and swagger. Her heart skidded and popped, a completely involuntary reaction. It seemed loud and felt like an earthquake aftershock, but when she glanced around no one else seemed to notice.

"Hi." He lifted a hand in greeting and everyone responded. "I saw the lights still on. Obviously this is the happening place on a weeknight in Thunder Canyon."

"That's for sure. Come see what Haley is drawing." Becky waved him over. "Look at how awesome these purses are. She even designed different linings, with a coordinating trim on the outside. Just small touches of it."

"I like the paisley," Kim commented.

"My favorite is the sun, crescent moon and stars," Jerilyn said.

"You're such a brainer geek." Becky looked at her friends and added, "I mean that in the best possible way."

The girls' chatter faded as Marlon moved closer to see what she was doing.

"Can I see?" he asked.

"Sure." Heart pounding in spite of her resolve not to react, she handed him the sketch pad.

While he flipped through it, she worked on getting her reaction in check. The spicy, clean scent of his aftershave wasn't making it easy.

Finally he looked at her. "These are good."

"Thanks."

"Good?" Becky sounded miffed. "That's the best adjective you can come up with?"

"They're awesome," Kim said again. "We'd buy them in a second."

"Haley knows how much I like her—designs," he added, his eyes dark with a thrilling intensity.

His slight hesitation before that last word had her pulse racing again.

"I do." Haley managed to keep her voice steady and normal. "He told me they have promise."

"I also said I'd like to send them to my assistant in L.A. Get her opinion on whether or not they're marketable."

"Of course they are." Jerilyn slid to the edge of the sofa in her earnestness. "They're different. Young. Fun and funky."

"Elegant, too," Becky added.

Kim came around and sat on the sofa arm,

presenting a united female front. "Haley's designs are really good. If your assistant doesn't get it, then you need a new assistant."

"Down, girl." He handed the pad to Haley, then backed up a step. "I said I'm on board. So far Haley hasn't given me the go-ahead."

Only because he'd kissed her and she freaked out. He'd invited her to dinner to discuss the possibility of doing business, but they didn't talk much after that kiss. It wasn't his fault she'd come unglued, then got sidetracked by insecurity and humiliation. Come to think of it, the idea of putting her designs out publicly brought up those same kinds of feelings.

"It's not an easy decision." She started putting her art supplies away in the pencil box.

"Why?" Kim demanded.

"Seems like a no-brainer." Jerilyn's dark eyes narrowed.

"You're scared." Becky nodded knowingly.

Haley looked at each girl in turn and finally nodded. "Yeah, I am. What if they're really awful?"

"That would mean we have no fashion sense," Kim said. "And that's just not possible."

"You don't understand," Haley protested.

"Sure we do." Jerilyn met her gaze. "It's like when I tried out for chorus at school. I didn't know if I was good enough. And I wanted so badly to make it because a lot of my friends belonged. I wanted it enough to risk someone telling me I was terrible. And this is high school where public is really public, if you know what I mean."

"They nailed you," Marlon said to Haley.

She saw laughter in his eyes and knew there would be no support from him. "But this is like putting my baby out there and giving the public a chance to say it's ugly."

"You need a name for the line," Marlon said, clearly unsympathetic to her insecurity. "A brand."

"Use your initials," Becky suggested. She picked up the last pencil—a green one—and wrote H-A on the sketch pad. "HA!"

"I like it." Marlon nodded approvingly. "All you have to do is give me the go-ahead."

A horn honked outside and through the window they could see a car at the curb.

"It's my mom," Kim said standing. "She's here to pick us up."

"Good." Haley was relieved that they had transportation after dark, and that she'd gotten a reprieve from the pressure.

Kim walked to the door with Jerilyn and Becky trailing behind. "See you, Roy. Austin. Bye, Marlon."

"Take a chance, Haley." Becky poked her head back in. "What have you got to lose?"

Then they were gone and Marlon watched from the window as they got safely into the car and drove away. Haley thought about what the girls had said and wondered who was mentoring whom. They were wise beyond their years.

Roy walked over and dropped into the chair. "Can we be done talking about chick stuff?"

"That works for me," Haley answered.

Austin joined them and shook hands with Marlon. "I hate to agree with Roy, but women's purses are boring. And the fact that you don't think so scares me." Her brother slid Marlon a skeptical look.

"It is boring," Marlon agreed. "But potentially lucrative. And I don't have to talk about it. That's what I have an assistant for."

"Lucrative? As in lots of money?" Austin was interested now.

"Some designers can get upwards of a thousand dollars for a handbag."

Austin's jaw dropped. "You're kidding me."

"No way," Roy said.

"Money is something I never joke about." Marlon looked dead serious.

"Me, either," Austin agreed. "Especially when you don't have any."

Haley knew what he was getting at and felt the need to explain. "Austin is talking about going to graduate school. To get a master's degree in engineering."

"Really?" Marlon looked impressed.

"Yeah." Austin rubbed a hand across his neck. "Green energy is the way of the future. We need to be oil-independent and I'd like to be a part of finding a way to do that in an environmentally responsible way."

"Good for you."

"Boring," Roy said.

Marlon reached over and ruffled the teen's hair. "Don't listen to him. If that's your dream, go for it."

"I'd like to, but—" Austin hesitated.

"The Anderson family budget spreadsheet doesn't have a column for graduate school tuition." Haley tried to make a joke, but it was hard when she knew how much her brother wanted this. It hurt that she couldn't give it to him.

Marlon folded his arms over his chest. "I could help. A loan maybe."

"Thanks," Haley said. "But we'll figure it out."

"A thousand dollars a pop?" Austin picked up the sketch pad and stared at her drawings in amazement. "I don't care what Haley says. Take this with my blessing. If someone says they're ugly, I'll beat them up for her."

Marlon laughed. "It's her decision. And nothing may come of it. There are no guarantees." He looked at her. "What do you say?"

She blew out a long breath and met his gaze, then echoed Becky. "What have I got to lose?"

"I'll send them to my assistant tomorrow." He nodded. "Good for you. There's no harm in trying."

Unlike giving in to her attraction for him. That could be incredibly harmful. She knew how it felt to lose someone she loved, how the sadness never completely went away. Marlon simply walked into the room and her body reacted as if she hadn't just warned herself not to care. Adrenaline-fueled hormones flooded her system and it was exciting. He was acting as if nothing was wrong between them and that felt good, too.

How was she going to be okay when he left town? How would she be all right when she couldn't look forward to him walking into the room anymore?

"I'm surprised that Roy left with Austin." Marlon looked at the front door the duo had just walked out of, then back at her.

Haley hit the Off switch on the computer and monitor. "I guess he needed a male bonding moment after all the chick talk without his wingman. C.J.'s dad had just picked him up before you came in and the girls and I started talking fashion."

"Has Roy given you any clue about where he's from or why he ran away?"

"Nothing." She turned away from the now dark monitor. "I tried to torture it out of him by forcing him to help me bake chocolate chip cookies."

"You made cookies?" He looked around the room.

"Sorry. The kids ate them all before you got here."

"And making them is an ordeal?"

"Yes for those of us who don't love baking. But this method of extracting information has sometimes been wildly successful."

"Austin doesn't count," Marlon said wryly.

"Darn." She turned serious. "It didn't count much with Roy, either. And he had the nerve to say I wasn't subtle, followed quickly by a declaration that no facts would be forthcoming."

"Too bad."

"Although he did say something about having to live with disappointment and I'm pretty sure he didn't mean the kids here who wouldn't have homemade cookies if we didn't bake."

Frowning, Marlon slid his fingertips into the pockets of his jeans. "He wasn't more specific?"

She shook her head. "For a teenage boy, disappointment could be anything from not getting a coveted video game to being shut down by the head cheerleader."

"I remember."

"Which one?"

"Both," he said ruefully. "You might not believe this, but I was fooled by a pretty face once."

"No. Really?" That shocked her. It didn't seem like bad ever happened to him. But the dark and angry expression on his face told her differently.

"I thought it was love at first sight, but she was after money." He shrugged. "I fell for it."

"Wow, Marlon, I don't know what to say." She wasn't happy he'd been hurt, but it made him more human somehow. Less godlike and untouchable.

"It was a long time ago."

"I guess she didn't get the Marlon magic?" she said, trying to tease a grin out of him.

It worked and his expression turned wry. "Not even a little bit. A guy never forgets something like that."

"Even an old guy like you?" Apparently she liked teasing him. The words just fell out of her mouth.

His gaze jumped to hers as he grinned. "Yeah. Even an old guy like me can remember that high school is like the wild wild west of hormones."

She hadn't been in high school for years, but every time he was near, her hormones zigged and zagged, dropped, rolled and ducked like a shootout at the OK Corral. "I've never heard it put quite like that."

"Doesn't make it any less true."

She sighed. "The thing is, Marlon, if he doesn't tell us something soon, I'm going to

210 TAMING THE MONTANA MILLIONAIRE

have to get Social Services involved. He's under eighteen."

"I know. And school will be starting soon. Covering for him too much longer isn't in his best interest."

"I just can't help feeling that it would be better if he volunteered the information instead of forcing it out of him."

"Teenage boys can be stubborn," he said.

"Is that the voice of experience?"

He looked at her. "I refuse to answer on the grounds that it may incriminate me."

"I'll take that as a yes." She smiled. It felt good. Being mad at him took a lot of negative energy. That flash of insight made her remember something else. "Roy made another comment."

"About himself?"

She shook her head. "He noticed the tension between us."

"Yeah, well…" He dragged his fingers through his hair. "You weren't very subtle about being peeved at me."

The kiss had embarrassed her and anger was the go-to emotion. She'd taken it out on him and that wasn't fair. "I'm sorry for the way I treated you."

He looked surprised, leaning more toward

shocked or stunned. "I don't quite know what to say."

She shrugged. "There's no excuse really. I've just had a lot on my mind and you were a handy target."

"No problem." There was warmth and sincerity in his expression when he added, "I was serious about helping Austin with graduate school expenses."

She smiled at the extraordinarily sweet and generous offer. And she was incredibly grateful that he went there instead of the real source of what was uppermost in her mind.

Him. MC. Major crush. Marlon Cates. Hottie and hometown hero.

When he left town after completing his community service, it might be easier on her if she were mad at him. But she didn't want the short amount of time he had left to be highlighted by anger and animosity. Teasing him was so much more fun.

"It's really kind of you to offer financial help, but Austin is looking into scholarships, grants and student loans first."

"If none of the above works out, you'll let me know?"

"Promise."

"Okay."

They smiled at each other and her pulse quickened as the blood seemed to rush to her head, pounding in her ears. It was time to go before she embarrassed herself again.

"It's getting late," she said. "I need to make sure everything is shut down and locked up."

"I'll give you a hand."

"Thanks."

They walked around turning off lights, TV and the video game. As Haley moved toward the back room, she heard the front door dead bolt slide home and knew Marlon had secured it. She grabbed her purse and keys from the closet, then hit the On switch for the angel night light in the powder room, making the dark not quite so absolute.

Marlon appeared in the doorway. "All set?"

"Yeah."

"I'll walk you to your truck."

"Okay."

There was a chilly breeze blowing when he followed her out and watched her secure the door. Her truck was parked under an outside light just a few steps from where they stood. Haley walked around to the driver's-side door and unlocked it. Marlon, standing behind her, reached around and opened it. She tossed her purse onto the passenger seat, then turned to say good-night.

"I appreciate you helping me out with my sketches."

"I'll come by in the morning and pick them up so I can overnight them to my assistant."

"Thanks for trying, even if nothing comes of it."

"Don't mention it. Whether you believe it or not, you're incredibly talented."

His deep, husky voice sent shivers over her skin. The truck was to her back and Marlon stood in front of her, blocking the wind. He was tall and broad, the sleeves of his T-shirt strained against the muscles bunching in his biceps. She instantly flashed on how good it had felt to be wrapped in his arms and a soft, yearning sound involuntarily slipped from her throat.

"Haley?" Intensity slid into his eyes making them darker, more dangerous.

"I—I should go—"

He reached out, cupping her cheek in his palm, and she leaned into the warmth, her eyelids drifting closed.

"Haley, I really want to kiss you…"

She opened her eyes and met his searching gaze. On some level she realized that he understood the last kiss had sparked the recent tension. This time, though, he was asking—and she couldn't have said no if her life depended on it.

"Okay," she whispered.

He slid the fingers of both hands into the hair around her face, brushed it off her cheeks. Then he lowered his head and softly touched his lips to hers. The achingly sweet contact made her eyes drift closed again as she sighed contentedly into his mouth. When his tongue touched hers, sparks of electricity arced through her and she opened wider. He dipped inside, stroking and caressing, making her breathe harder, faster, until she could hardly breathe at all.

His hand dropped to her waist and squeezed gently. Almost of their own accord, her arms tangled around his neck and she lifted up on her toes, trying to get closer. He pulled her snugly against him and held her there as he nibbled kisses over the corner of her mouth, jaw and neck. She could hear his own raspy breathing and joy surged through her.

They were as close as a man and woman could be. Almost, she thought as longing sliced through her, knotting uncomfortably in her chest. She snuggled and squirmed against him, instinctively trying to get nearer, and felt the hard ridge of his desire. He wanted her, she thought. And she wanted him right back. Her body throbbed with a powerful need, a feeling like she'd never felt before and had never known was there.

Marlon had awakened it and she wanted to know everything there was to know about being a woman. She slid her fingers into the hair at his nape and brushed her thumb over his neck. His deep groan of yearning made her heart sing. She wanted to touch him again, explore the wide expanse of his chest, the bare skin beneath his shirt. And she wanted him to do the same to her.

Just then the headlights of a car pulling into the far side of the lot flashed over them and they jumped apart. Both of them were breathing hard and Marlon hunched protectively over her, hiding her.

The knee-jerk reaction was sweet, but unnecessary, although five minutes longer and there might have been a whole lot more to hide.

"You better go." Marlon dragged his fingers through his hair.

"Can I drop you off at The Hitching Post?"

Her voice was a breathless, wanton whisper that didn't sound at all like her.

There was a slight hesitation before he shook his head. "The walk will do me good."

"Are you sure, because it's on my way—"

He settled his hands at her waist and lifted her into the truck. "Go, before it's too late."

He shut the door, not letting her question what that meant. But she knew. If he asked her to his room, she would go without a second's thought. She wanted him to make love to her, make her a woman. She might be a naive virgin, but the ache deep inside her didn't need explanation.

More important, the longing to be with him was impossible to ignore.

Chapter Eleven

Haley had never been more grateful for small-town traffic patterns than she was on the drive home. It was late, and she passed only a handful of cars and trucks. That was fortunate since part of her attention was focused on the aftereffects of kissing Marlon. This time was so much better because she didn't freeze up and freak out.

Her spirits were flying and her body hummed. Every part of her felt keyed up in the most wonderful way. Her nerve endings were highly sensitive. But the best part? She couldn't ever remember being this happy.

Marlon had wanted her.

She was sure of it.

For some reason, he hadn't wanted to take things to third plate, or home base, or whatever the slang was for going all the way. She was sure that's what he'd meant when he told her to go before it was too late. But she was way past late and had a lot of catching up to do.

And she wanted to catch up with Marlon.

She'd had a thing for him as long as she could remember and that teenage kiss had made her want more even then. But the timing had been all wrong. Now wasn't much better; he was leaving town soon. All the more reason to catch up while she could.

This time when he left, she didn't want any regrets. No one got through life without them, but some you could control and making love with Marlon fell into that column.

She was a grown up now and knew the score. No expectations for tomorrow, just live in the now. Of course her mother had advised her to wait for the right man—someone she cared about who cared about her. The L-word was never spoken, just implied during "the talk" all those years ago.

There wasn't a doubt in Haley's mind that

she and Marlon cared about each other. It felt very right for him to be the first.

And only.

"Not going there," she muttered to herself.

No expectations; no promises. There was just now.

And that's when Haley made up her mind.

She was going back to town and knock on Marlon's door upstairs at The Hitching Post. If she was wrong about him wanting her, so be it. She was getting pretty good at surviving humiliation. Regrets, not so much. There was a very good chance that this state of wanting and not having him would make her implode.

Since she was almost home, she decided to stop in and let Austin and Angie know what she was doing. Well, not precisely what, just that she had to go back to Thunder Canyon and they shouldn't worry.

Haley pulled into the driveway and parked the truck beside her brother's small, aging compact, then grabbed her purse. When she walked up to the front door, she heard male voices. Loud voices. Arguing. She went inside and the chaotic scene matched the feelings bouncing through her, but for a very different reason.

Austin was in Roy's face. "I know what I saw."

"You don't have a clue, dude."

"Don't call me dude."

"Stop, Austin," Angie cried. "It's not what you think."

"You put the moves on my sister." Austin poked Roy in the chest.

Angie grabbed her brother's arm. "He didn't. How many times do I have to tell you?"

Haley dropped her purse just inside the door. "What's going on?"

Without looking away from Roy, Austin said, "He made a pass at Angie."

"No way," Roy protested. "Haley, I wouldn't do that."

Angie met her gaze. "He's like a little brother. We're friends."

"Then why was he on top of you when I walked in the room?" Austin demanded.

"We were wrestling for the cookies," Roy said defensively, blue eyes blazing.

Haley saw the empty plastic cookie container on the rug in the front room, by the couch. The cookies were broken and chocolate chips ground into the carpet. Roy's T-shirt was ripped and Austin's sports shirt was only partially tucked into his jeans. She was no forensics expert, but it didn't take top-notch detective skills to see the two had scuffled. Quickly scanning their faces, she saw no evidence that punches were thrown. So far it was only pushing and shoving.

A muscle in Austin's jaw bunched. "You're taking advantage of Haley's kindness. In return you're hitting on my other sister. You're not getting away with it. I'm not going to stand by and let some jerk I know nothing about hurt my family."

"I'm not doing that—" Roy moved closer and Austin shoved him back.

When that escalated to grappling, Haley snapped out of her shock. She moved forward and with Angie's help shoved between them.

"Stop it right now." She shouted to be heard over the grunting and heavy breathing from exertion.

"He started it," the teen said.

"I stopped it before you could start anything," Austin argued.

"Do something, Haley," Angie begged. "Austin's gone all macho and over-protective."

"Someone has to." Austin's dark eyes snapped with anger. Breathing hard, he looked at Haley and said, "What do you know about this kid?"

"I know he needs help," she defended.

"And what if he's playing you? He won't say where he's from or why he won't go home. He could be taking advantage of your soft heart. A user. Someone has to look out for you."

"I can take care of myself," Haley said.

"Me, too," Angie chimed in. "I don't need Rambo coming to the rescue."

Austin shook his head. "That's not the way it looked to me."

"I have no reason not to believe or trust Roy," Haley said. "Let's all take a deep breath and calm down."

"So you're taking his side over your own brother?" Austin looked even angrier.

"I'm not taking anyone's side. There's no side to take. It was a misunderstanding."

"When are you going to wake up?" Austin challenged. "Make him tell you where he's from or toss his backside out."

"What if I do that and Roy gets hurt?" Haley demanded. "Where would you be now if people had treated you that way when you were a teenager with problems?"

"Are you ever going to let me forget that?"

he demanded. "Just so we're clear, you're not my mother. I grew up, got my head on straight. It's what a guy does." Austin glared at Roy, then turned his fierce expression back to her. "You and Angie are way too trusting."

"I don't need anyone telling me what to do." Angie looked first at her, then Austin. "Especially my brother. Just because you have a bachelor's degree doesn't mean you have a brain. I don't need you fighting my battles. I'll give my trust to whoever I darn well please."

Haley would give anything to have Marlon here, and his understanding of the male point of view along with him. Everything that came out of her mouth was wrong and seemed to make this situation even more tense.

With an effort, she pulled the tatters of her patience together. "Saying derogatory things to your brother isn't helping, Angie."

"And neither is he," she argued, pointing at her sibling.

Haley looked at her sister. "Doesn't he get points for the sentiment? He's just trying to be a good big brother."

Angie shook her head. "He's interfering in my life. Don't even talk to me about points."

"How about the point on top of your head?" Austin snarled.

"Very funny. Is that the best you've got?"

"I've saved the good stuff," Austin retorted. "Get ready. Here it comes—"

"Look, dude, don't pick on Angie," Roy interrupted.

The two made a threatening move toward each other until Haley put a palm on each of their chests to keep them separated. There was so much testosterone in the room it was a wonder she could stand her ground at all. And again she wished Marlon was there to back her up.

When had she started to rely on him so much?

Right now she couldn't think about the downside of that. First she had to get a cease-fire from these two.

"Everyone stand down," she ordered. "Take five and we'll talk about this without punching and yelling."

"I'm not a kid. Don't even tell me to use my words." Angie glared at her. "Let me say this one more time. We're just friends. Austin is being an ass. I'm a grown-up and don't need you hovering. You need to back off."

She stalked out of the room and moments later her bedroom door slammed.

Haley felt as if she'd been punched in the stomach. "Okay, she needs to cool off. Roy— Austin—"

"She's right. Talking is a bunch of crap." Austin stared angrily over her head at Roy. "I manned up. I did what I thought was right. I make my own decisions. You need to let go, Haley." He left and the house shook when his bedroom door crashed closed.

Double punch to the gut. She was reeling, almost as if the words had been physical blows. Why was she suddenly the bad guy? She'd taken care of them when she was just a kid herself. What had she done that was so wrong?

If they wanted space, they could have it. But Roy needed help and she wouldn't let him down.

"That went well." She blew out a long breath. "Kind of makes you glad that I'm not part of America's diplomatic corps."

"Whatever." The teen flopped on the sofa, his body still vibrating with pent-up anger.

Now what? Roy had been sleeping on an air mattress in Austin's room, but that didn't seem like a good idea.

"I think for tonight it would be best if you spent the night on the couch." When he looked at her and shrugged, she said, "I'll get some bedding for you."

Without waiting for an answer, she left him and went down the hall to the linen closet for sheets, blanket and pillow. On her way she passed closed doors and couldn't help feeling left out in the cold. And just the tiniest bit sorry for herself.

All she'd wanted was to smooth over the incident and be one big happy family. Instead her family, the only people she had in this world, was mad at her. She'd never felt more alone in her life.

She remembered the warm feel of Marlon's arms around her and desperately wanted to go to him. But she couldn't leave. If World War III broke out again, someone had to be Switzerland. That made her feel even more alone.

The morning after kissing Haley Marlon was wound so tight he felt ready to explode. It had probably been the most boneheaded move he'd ever made. His body was revved and sent his mind to a place where he longed to spend the night with her in his arms, his mouth on hers.

Just like that his body tensed all over again. He remembered her contented sigh, the needy little sounds she'd made. The short walk from ROOTS to The Hitching Post hadn't come close to taking the edge off his need. It would be right there when he saw her again later this morning.

He still didn't know how he'd come up with the willpower to turn down her offer of a ride, but somehow he'd resisted the almost irresistible temptation. Maybe because he knew he'd invite her up to his room. Possibly he hadn't wanted to hear her say no. Or yes. Or tell him yet again that he didn't do commitment. The problem was, now that she'd put the idea of commitment in his head, it wouldn't leave him alone. And she was the only one he could think about.

But that was crazy. Maybe not as nuts as falling for a woman's con to get money out of him, but nuts all the same. Haley's life was here in Thunder Canyon and his wasn't. He was going back to L.A. When had the initial impatience to get his license back turned into regret at having to leave Haley?

He paced his room, trying to pin down the moment, all the while knowing it wouldn't change anything. Stopping beside the king-size bed, he couldn't help picturing Haley there with him, which couldn't—wouldn't—happen. Somehow he knew that if it did, walking away from her would be like ripping his heart out.

Poetic thoughts like that were pretty lame for a guy who'd never been accused of having a sensitive side. And all this pacing and regret was just putting off the inevitable—seeing her. She'd be working the breakfast shift downstairs. There were other places in town to eat, but not as good. And sooner or later he would have to see her because he still had community service hours to perform.

"Might as well get it over with," he said to the empty room. At least he'd gotten her sketches off to L.A. first thing that morning. "I can tell her that my assistant will be looking at them this time tomorrow."

He was bracing himself for the punch-to-the-gut sensation Haley always gave him when there was a knock on his door. The sound was startling because he never had visitors.

He opened the door, and got the punch-to-the-gut feeling when he saw who was there. "Haley."

"Hi, Marlon. Sorry to bother you."

"You're not." At least not in a way he could share. "I'm glad you stopped by. I wanted you to know that I overnighted your sketches to my assistant first thing this morning. I—" He noticed something on her face that clued him in. She hadn't come about her drawings. "Is something wrong?"

She twisted her fingers together. "Is Roy here by any chance?"

"No. I haven't seen him since he left ROOTS last night with Austin."

The hopeful expression on her expressive face turned to disappointment, then worry. "Okay. Thanks."

"Wait." He reached out and grabbed her arm when she started to turn away. "Why are you looking for him?"

"He was gone this morning."

"I see." Marlon leaned a shoulder against the doorjamb and slid his fingertips into the pockets of his jeans. "Maybe he went home."

"I think he would have said something, don't you?"

"He's a runaway. By definition that makes him unpredictable."

"I think that's part of the age. The thing is, I thought we connected. And for him to leave without a note or anything feels wrong to me. That's why I thought he might be here with you."

There was something she wasn't telling him. He'd bet money on it. And when had he gotten to know her that well? "Did something happen before he took off?"

Her gaze jumped to his and she was chewing on her bottom lip. Finally she said, "There was an awful scene last night."

He straightened away from the door frame. It didn't sound like this was something she'd want to discuss in the hallway. "Come in. Tell me what happened."

She passed him and walked into the room. They were alone, but this wasn't the way he'd pictured having her all to himself.

"When I got home last night," she started, "Roy and Austin were arguing."

The two had seemed like best buds when they'd left the teen center. "What happened?"

"I guess Austin walked in on Roy and Angie goofing around and assumed the worst."

"That Roy was hitting on his sister?" he guessed.

She nodded. "They insisted they're just friends and Austin was overreacting. I tried to get everyone to shake hands and apologize, but the next thing I knew they were all telling me to get off their case and butt out."

"Roy, too?"

She shook her head. "He was back to his default response."

"Whatever?" he guessed.

"That's the one," she said grimly. "This morning my brother and sister were barely speaking to me or each other. And Roy was just gone."

"Have you checked with C.J.? Or Jerilyn? Or some of the other kids from the center?"

"Not yet." Worry clouded her eyes. "I was hoping I wouldn't have to because I'd find him hanging out here with you. But I'll start making phone calls. Thanks, Marlon. Sorry to bother you."

"Stop saying that. You're not bothering me. I want to help." He dragged his fingers through his hair. "What if no one has heard from him?"

"I'll keep looking."

"Why?"

"Because he ran away from home and now he's run away from me. I feel responsible."

"Haley, you did nothing but try to help that kid. It's not your fault."

"Maybe not, but he could be out there

alone. Just because he's a guy doesn't mean he's not at the mercy of predators—" Her voice caught and she pressed her full lips together.

"Do you have a plan?" he asked, wanting to fix this for her. He wanted to be her knight in shining armor and chase the apprehension from her face. He knew it was stupid, but that didn't make the feeling go away.

"Yeah. If he's nowhere to be found in Thunder Canyon, I'm going to Billings."

That surprised him. "Why?"

"When he was hanging out at the center with the other teens, I overheard him say he has a friend there."

"Did he happen to mention the name of this friend?"

"No, but—"

"Haley, that's like spitting into the wind."

"I don't care." She threw up her arms in frustration. "Sitting around isn't an option."

Determination was a good quality, but Marlon wished she had a little less. He hated the idea of her going all alone. As she'd so graphically stated, there were predators out there. Unlike Roy, she wasn't a guy.

"Is there any way to talk you out of this?"

"Unless you've been lying to me and Roy is

hiding under the bed… No. You can't change my mind."

"That's what I thought you'd say." He grabbed his wallet and room key from the desk. "In that case, I'm going with you."

"That's not necessary. You should open the center—"

"The kids will survive if it doesn't open for a day. I'll help you make phone calls. It will be faster. If no one's heard from him, we'll cruise Thunder Canyon and look for him." He held up his hand to stop her when she opened her mouth. "Two pairs of eyes are better than one and you're driving."

"Really, I can handle this."

Without acknowledging her protest, he continued, "If our search doesn't produce any results, we'll go to Billings together. I'm not letting you look for him by yourself."

"I won't be," she protested. "My best friend, Elise Clifton, lives there. She knows the town and can give me a hand."

He shook his head, determined to out-stubborn her. "That doesn't solve the problem of you driving there alone. What if you have a flat tire? A problem with your truck? It's not getting any younger."

"I'm used to handling stuff."

"So you've said."

He couldn't refute that she'd had to handle stuff. Life had smacked her down, but she didn't stay there. She thumbed her nose at fate, picked herself up and thrived in spite of everything. She was a beautiful, talented woman who was also determined, obstinate, persistent and caring. The problem of her going alone wasn't hers. It was his.

He wasn't used to worrying about anyone, but that didn't seem to stop the protective feeling rolling through him. He didn't like worrying about her and was going along whether she liked it or not.

Staying here in Thunder Canyon while she went to look for an impulsive teenager all by herself wasn't an option.

"Here's the deal, Haley. We can stand here and argue, wasting precious time. Or you can give in gracefully and let me help you cut the work in half. Because I'm not taking no for an answer." He rested his hands on his hips and stared her down. "So what's it going to be?"

She took his measure for several moments, then said, "Okay. You can help."

"Good choice. Let's go find the bonehead."

She grinned for the first time since he'd

opened the door and made him feel like he'd given her the moon and stars.

Later he would worry about why that reaction was a bad thing.

Chapter Twelve

Haley could admit to herself that she was happy Marlon had accompanied her to Billings, but never out loud for him to hear. For one thing, nothing good would come of it. And she had to focus on finding Roy. The man she'd believed Marlon to be just a few short weeks ago would never have inconvenienced himself for anyone. She'd learned he wasn't that man.

But this man could break her heart if she wasn't careful.

They climbed back into her truck after talking to a representative for the Billings police and Marlon said, "Now what?"

"I'm thinking."

Not entirely about finding the teen, but that would stay her secret. "The cops weren't much help."

"They'll do what they can. Keeping an eye out for anyone meeting Roy's description is something. And the sketch you did of our boy was a pretty good likeness. Distributing the copies they made to patrol officers may produce results."

"It doesn't feel like enough," she grumbled, glancing at him in the passenger seat.

His expression was wry. "Unfortunately they can't mobilize a task force for every runaway kid. It happens too often and is usually nothing more than a grounded teenager hiding out to punish a parent who dared not be their friend."

"And who really gets punished?" She knew how awful it felt to worry about someone you love. But he was right, although that didn't make her feel better.

"I know you're concerned, but there's no reason to believe he won't be fine. Roy will probably have kids someday. The fruit doesn't fall far from the tree. DNA and all that. He'll almost certainly have one a lot like him. What goes around comes around and he'll live to regret this. Live is the operative word." He reached over and squeezed her shoulder reassuringly.

She wasn't reassured, but his touch made her concentrate on catching her breath instead of the lost boy. Was it only hours ago that she'd made up her mind to go to Marlon's room and finish what he'd started with that kiss in the ROOTS parking lot? It felt like a lifetime ago. Even worse, another missed opportunity.

She sighed. "We can phone shelters. They might be able to give us leads about where homeless teens tend to hang out."

He nodded. "We need a local phone book."

"I know just where to find one."

She started the truck and pulled out into traffic. A short time later, they stopped in front of a book store. It was located on a quaint street with retail shops sporting western facades and wooden walkways, not unlike the ones in Thunder Canyon.

Marlon looked at the storefront. "Books and More?"

"Elise works here. I called her. She's expecting us."

"And she'll have a phone book," he guessed.

Haley nodded. "And she knows the town.

She might have some ideas of her own about where to look for a teenager who doesn't want to be found."

They got out of the truck and walked to the door. The bell above it rang when the door was opened. Haley had been here before, managing to take a couple of days off to visit her friend. But it never seemed long enough. And suddenly excitement shot through her along with acute impatience.

She glanced anxiously around at book shelves lining the store's perimeter and displays of the current bestsellers straight ahead. Beyond that were rows of genres—mystery, thrillers—and her personal favorite—romance.

Before she could decide which way to go, a blue-eyed blonde in navy slacks and a white blouse moved from behind one of the racks. Instantly a pleased smile lit up her pretty face.

"Haley!"

There was hugging, talking at the same time, and laughing.

"It's so good to see you, Haley. How long has it been?"

"Too long." She looked up at the man beside her. "You remember Marlon Cates."

Elise nodded. "You're not easy to forget."

"Should I be scared or flattered?" His expression was half-teasing, half-wary.

"Both." She grinned. "I was a year behind you in school. You always seemed to travel with an entourage. And having a twin brother for a wingman didn't hurt. Everyone wanted to be your friend."

"I'm not quite sure how to respond to that."

Elise laughed. "You don't have to say anything."

She and Elise were the same height, same age, although the other woman looked younger and always had. The small brown birthmark on the bridge of her nose, right side, hadn't gone away. She watched her friend's easy exchange with Marlon and waited for a flash of jealousy, like she'd felt when he'd talked to Erin Castro. But it never came. Maybe because he was treating Elise like a little sister.

Haley felt guilty about Roy taking off in the first place, but the silver lining of that particular cloud was the chance to see her friend.

"Elise, you look so good. Your hair's different. Longer." The golden blond strands brushed her shoulders and barely curved under.

"That's my cue," Marlon said.

Haley glanced up. "For what?"

"To leave. So you can engage in girl talk."

"Have you had lunch yet?" Elise asked.

It was after one o'clock and Haley had forgotten about eating, but her stomach chose that moment to growl. She put a hand on her abdomen and laughed ruefully. "That would be no."

"There's a cute little café two doors down. They make a great club sandwich."

"Anyplace is fine." Haley glanced at Marlon again. "You have to eat."

"I saw a fast food place up the street. I'll just grab a burger there." He looked at Elise. "If I can borrow your phone book, I'll make some calls and see if I can get some leads on our boy." He snapped his fingers. "And if you have a copy machine, I'll duplicate a sketch Haley made and circulate it."

"That's a good idea," Haley said. "But I should help you."

He shook his head. "Give yourself a break. Take an hour. I insist."

She knew once he'd made up his mind, trying to change it would be as impossible as moving the mountains that surrounded Thunder Canyon. So she gave in gracefully. "Okay, then."

Elise nodded toward the back of the store. "Let me just tell my boss I'm going to lunch."

Fifteen minutes later she and Elise were sitting at a round table covered with a red checkered cloth. Club sandwiches and fries nestled in white plastic baskets and diet sodas were sitting in front of them and they dug in eagerly.

"So how are you?" Haley wiped her mouth with the paper napkin.

"Good. I love working at the bookstore. When it's not busy I can bury myself in a book."

Escape, Haley thought. And her friend had good reasons for wanting to. "What's new?"

Elise chewed thoughtfully, then her blue eyes lit up. "I'm going to be an aunt. Grant and his wife, Stephanie, are expecting a baby."

"That's great," Haley said. "I hadn't heard."

"I'm sure you will." Her friend grinned. "Nothing stays a secret in Thunder Canyon."

"That's so true. This is yummy," Haley said, picking up her second triangle of sandwich.

"So is Marlon." Elise's blue eyes danced with the teasing. "What's up with that?"

"With what?"

"Don't play dumb, Haley. This is me and I will not be distracted. You and Marlon? A relationship?"

"There's no relationship—"

Haley's automatic denial died on her lips. She was so used to pushing aside her feelings, putting on a perky face, pretending everything was perfect. But this was Elise, the one person she could always open her heart to. The friend she'd always been able to talk to and unburden herself. Maybe because they both shared deep personal losses. Elise's father had been murdered on his ranch years earlier. When life in Thunder Canyon became too painful, her mom had moved them to Billings. And when Haley's mom died in the car accident, she'd finally understood her friend's soul-deep sadness and their bond deepened. For whatever reason, this was a rare and precious opportunity to talk to her friend, face-to-face. No phone. And no email, which was even less satisfying.

"Okay." Haley picked up a fry and took a bite. "I wouldn't call it a relationship. Not what you're implying. We're friends, I guess."

"So the spark I saw between you was just static electricity?" Elise hardly looked older than eighteen, but she missed nothing.

"Okay. He kissed me."

"Really?"

"Yeah. Twice."

"Does that tally include the one at the football fundraiser six years ago?"

Haley had told her all about that, including a blow-by-blow of the heartbreak and disappointment that followed when he didn't call. "Okay," she confessed. "Three times."

"And?"

"And nothing." She explained about him losing his driver's license and the community service that kept them practically joined at the hip. Temporarily. "He's going back to L.A. Soon."

"And your heart is going to break again." It wasn't a question.

"Not this time. He hasn't promised anything and I know he's leaving. Older and wiser." She shrugged and took a sip from her diet soda.

"Just because you know the score it doesn't mean you can keep your emotions in check. It's not like ordering your dog to sit, stay, play dead."

How she wished her feelings were dead, but just the opposite was true. Emotions were alive, well, thriving out of control.

"I know."

"Have you slept with him?" Elise asked.

If anyone else had asked, Haley would have been shocked and embarrassed. Elise knew that she'd never had sex. "No."

"Do you want to?"

"Yes," she said simply. No point in lying. Her friend always saw through her.

"So you really do care." There was gentle understanding in Elise's soft voice.

"How did you know?"

"If you didn't, you wouldn't even consider going to bed with him." Sympathy and understanding were soft in her friend's blue eyes. "Maybe Marlon is the reason you've waited this long."

She was right. Warm feelings for this wonderful friend welled up and tears filled her eyes. She felt a little less alone because there was someone in this world who knew her so well.

"I miss you so much." She reached over and squeezed Elise's hand. "I wish we could talk like this more often."

"Well, I'll be back in Thunder Canyon for the holidays. We'll get together then."

"Christmas seems so far away."

"The time will fly," Elise promised.

"I could be more patient if it wasn't going to be a temporary visit. When Grant and Stephanie's baby is born, you're going to want to be close to your niece or nephew. A good reason to make it a permanent move. Don't blame me for keeping my fingers crossed."

"They're your fingers, but—" Deep sadness dimmed the sparkle in Elise's eyes. "I really can't live there. Too many bad memories."

Haley nodded, knowing all about the awful things that had happened. But she couldn't help hoping that the next visit would change her friend's mind about making it a move back for good. She was going to need the comfort of talks like this when Marlon went back to his regularly scheduled life and took her heart with him.

"It won't kill you to have some dinner, Haley."

Marlon lounged in the open doorway to her room. The search had taken all afternoon. They'd made phone calls, tacked up copies of his sketch all over town and driven around looking for Roy without success. It was getting late and he could see how tired she was. Her exhaustion would make the trip back to

Thunder Canyon an ordeal. Without a license, he couldn't take over the driving for her.

Finally he'd made an executive decision and reserved two rooms for the night at a hotel. He'd known it was the right decision when she didn't fight him on it.

After a trip to the local Walmart for necessities, he'd come next door to convince Haley that a hunger strike wouldn't help find the teenager and would only hurt her in the long run.

"It feels wrong," she finally answered.

"Are you afraid you'll have fun?" he challenged.

"Of course not—" She stopped, a puzzled look on her face as she tried to figure out what, if anything, she'd admitted.

"Then you don't want to spend time with me."

"I do, it's just—" Again she stopped, frowning.

Marlon definitely wanted to spend time with her. He just wished there wasn't a dark cloud hovering over this trip, that she could be carefree and forget about responsibility for a while. He wanted to give her that before it was time to go.

He moved farther into the room—a duplicate of his. There was a king-size bed covered with a blue-green patterned comforter. The walls were cream-colored and dark wood nightstands bracketed the bed. A bathroom was to the right by the door. It was your basic, generic hotel room.

He should know. He'd stayed in what felt like a million of them, traveling around by himself. But just having Haley next door made it different, special and he wanted to do something for her. Buying her a nice dinner seemed right.

"What is it, Haley?" he asked again. "There's nothing more you can do tonight. We've left cell phone numbers with everyone possible. If anyone has information about Roy, they'll call. Let's stand down. Just for a little while."

Her brown eyes darkened with the conflict raging inside her. Finally her gaze lifted to his. "Is this one of those times when you're not taking no for an answer?"

"You noticed that about me?"

"Didn't have to notice. You're not shy about announcing it." She shook her head and muttered, "Darn sales personality."

"I know." He grinned as he took her elbow and guided her from the room. "Gotta love it."

"It's very irritating."

"Part of my charm." At the end of the hall, he pushed the down elevator button.

"You call it charm. I say pigheaded, obstinate and inflexible."

"Takes one to know one. And my mother calls it perseverance." When the doors whispered open, they stepped into the car. "She always said it would be a good quality in an adult. A kid? Not so much."

"Your mom is a smart lady."

"I take after her." That finally merited a smile. She'd made him work, but it was worth the reward.

There was a nice restaurant right next door and this time he didn't make the mistake of kissing her on the way. Although the memory of her response to his mouth on hers last night hinted at a more positive outcome.

They walked inside the place, which had candlelight and white tablecloths. The hostess greeted, then seated them in a quiet corner of the uncrowded dining room. It was impossible not to notice the romantic surroundings.

Haley looked beautiful in unforgiving sunshine, but by candlelight she took his breath away. Her brown hair was loose and teased her shoulders and cheeks, making him want to bury his fingers in the silky softness. This place had probably been a mistake. Somewhere called Bubba's Burgers and Beans would have been noisy and loud, not at all suited to passionate thoughts. Although he wasn't sure even that atmosphere would have completely erased his growing need to touch her.

A waitress in black pants and pristine white blouse appeared beside them. "My name is Claire and I'll be your server tonight. Can I get you a cocktail or glass of wine?"

Marlon looked at Haley and the frown told him that's where she drew the line. Fun was one thing, but keeping a clear head because of why they were here took priority.

"Iced tea for me," he said.

"Make it two," said Haley.

"Coming right up." She handed them menus and left to get their drinks.

"No beer?" One corner of Haley's full mouth lifted.

"Gotta keep a clear focus. Just in case."

The approval shining in her eyes made him feel as if he'd just gone to the head of the class. It was a potent reaction and that was dangerous. Possibly leading to promises he wasn't sure he could keep. He didn't want to risk doing anything to lead her on. There wouldn't be a repeat of not keeping his word.

He opened his menu and had to force himself to read the choices. The time for him to go back to L.A. was approaching far too quickly and it felt as if he couldn't look at her long enough. Hard enough.

"So what are you having?" he asked, not really seeing the words. He chanced a glance and she was nervously chewing on her lip. "What?"

"The prices…" She glanced up.

"I can afford it."

"You don't have to."

He wondered if she'd ever been to a restaurant more upscale than The Hitching Post. He doubted it. No one seemed to know if she dated. The jerk in college probably hadn't taken her anywhere fancy. This might be his only chance to do something for the woman who took care of everyone else.

"If you don't order whatever you want, regardless of the cost, I'm getting you the most expensive dinner they have."

Her eyes widened. "There are things listed without the cost. It says market price."

"Live dangerously."

"Really?"

He was. Just by being here. "Yeah."

Claire came back with the drinks and said, "Are you ready to order? Or do you need a few minutes?"

"I'm ready," Haley said. "Petite filet mignon, medium rare, with a baked potato and house salad."

"Good choice," said Marlon. "I'll have the same."

"Coming right up."

Fifteen minutes later they were digging into their meals. The pleasured expression on Haley's face was a mixed blessing. It was good to see her enjoying an experience that he took for granted. Bad because blood flow went south of his belt as thoughts of other ways to pleasure her refused to leave him alone. He was a jerk and the seventh level of hell wouldn't be low enough for him.

When she declared herself too full to eat another bite, half her steak still sat on her plate. He finished it for her.

"I had a feeling that would happen," he said.

"Is that why you ordered the smaller cut? Because the women you take to dinner leave half of theirs?"

And just like that the sad, guarded expression was back in her eyes. Before he could ask her about it, Claire returned and they declined dessert, so she took his credit card.

"What's wrong, Haley?" he finally said.

"I was just wondering if Roy had dinner tonight."

The "women he took to dinner" remark told him it was more than that, but he didn't want to go there. Instead, he asked, "Why do you do that?"

"What?"

"Shut down the fun. Punishing yourself doesn't do anything except make you feel sad. It doesn't change the fact that bad stuff happens and none of it is within your control."

She slapped her cloth napkin on the table and glared. "You don't think I already know that?"

"I know you know," he said. "More than anyone you should understand how important it is to live in the moment. You can't walk around waiting for the other shoe to fall."

"That's easy for you to say. When you went to college, left home for the first time, no one called a few weeks later to tell you your mother was dead. You didn't have to rush home in a state of shock to a brother and sister even more traumatized than you.

"One day you're the oldest child and the next you're parenting the only family you have left in the world." She drew in a shuddering breath. "Do you have any idea what it's like to be dumped into a responsibility that you didn't ask for and in no way deserve?"

"You did an unbelievable job," he said sincerely.

"If that's true, I couldn't have done it without Ben Walters. He was like the father I never had."

"Even more than you know."

"What does that mean?" she demanded. "Why don't you like him?"

"I think you've got that reversed."

He hadn't meant to say anything to her, but couldn't be sorry he had. It was important before he left to let her know that when he'd said he was going to call her, he'd fully intended to do just that. He needed her to know that he wasn't a heartless player, that she was wrong when she'd mocked his commitment capability. He wanted to clear the air.

"Six years ago I kissed you at the football carnival and told you I'd call. Somehow Ben Walters found out." He shrugged. "No secrets in a small town."

"I don't understand."

"Ben warned me to stay away from you. That you weren't my type and he wasn't too old to make me sorry if I hurt you."

"Ben threatened you?"

"It was a guy thing. And he was right to do it." Marlon watched her jaw drop. "For what it's worth, recently he told me he was wrong about me."

"I never knew that." Surprise chased the sadness from her eyes. "All this time I've been thinking the worst about you."

"So what you said about commitment not being one of my strengths…" he teased.

"I'm sorry."

He wasn't looking for an apology, just clarification. And he definitely didn't want to make her feel bad. "Please don't look like that. I just thought you should know why I didn't call back then. I didn't mean to hurt you."

And if there was a God in heaven he wouldn't hurt her now. Or ever.

"I believe that," she said. "But it happened. And that wasn't the worst. It's hard for me to live in the moment, let my guard down and have fun. Taking a chance, moving forward… that hasn't worked out so well for me—"

Her voice broke and her lips trembled. She

put her hand over her mouth, looking completely destroyed by the collapse of her composure. Without another word, she stood up and hurried out of the restaurant.

Marlon quickly signed the credit card receipt Claire had unobtrusively slipped on the table, then followed Haley. He couldn't stand to see her look like that.

But it was worse to stand back and do nothing. She wasn't alone; he was there. The least he could do was hold her while she cried.

Chapter Thirteen

Haley wasn't sure how she managed to find her way to her room, what with tears blurring her eyes. But she did, and stopped outside her door, fumbling in her jeans pocket for the card key.

It had been six years since her mother died. She'd managed to get everything under control. She was under control, always. So, what had made her melt down like that after so long?

Why tonight?

Why with Marlon?

Just thinking his name brought a fresh wave of emotion and she couldn't see to get her key in the slot. It didn't help that her hand was shaking.

"Damn it," she said brokenly.

"Haley?"

She'd felt him behind her even before he'd spoken. All she wanted was to be alone and have her little scene in the privacy of her room.

"Please go away." Was that too much to ask?

"I can't leave you like this."

Apparently it was. "I'm fine."

"All evidence to the contrary. What's wrong?"

Too much to put into words. How could she tell him that she'd lost it because the future couldn't include him when they both wanted different things?

Just like that a fresh wave of tears trickled down her cheeks and she pressed a hand over her mouth to stifle a sob.

"Nothing's wrong."

"I don't believe you." His hands on her shoulders turned her. "Come here."

He wrapped his arms around her and pressed her close. She rested her cheek on his chest, comforted by the steady beat of his heart, the warmth of his body.

"Don't cry, Haley. We'll find Roy."

"I know."

It was easier to let him think that was the problem than explain she wasn't as selfless as he thought. This emotion was all about her. "I didn't mean to spoil the evening. You didn't need to follow me back."

But she couldn't manage to be sorry that he had.

"I can't stand to see you so upset. I had to make sure you were okay or do something to fix it."

"Stand down." She sniffled. "I'll dry."

He backed her up a step and looked down. "Promise?"

"Yes."

They stared at each other for several moments and she knew the exact moment he went from comfort mode to something else entirely. His brown eyes darkened and a muscle in his jaw tensed.

"You need to go in your room." His voice was deep, dangerous.

In a brief, blinding flash of clarity she knew that this was one of those turning points in life. A place where choices happened along with regrets. She could choose to live and look back with pride or duck and run and be sorry about it for the rest of her days. Was it only last night that she'd planned to go to his room and take the step? Fate had given her a second chance and she couldn't throw it away.

"No," she said. "Take me to your room."

Surprise jumped into his eyes, but the darkness was back a moment later. "That's a bad idea."

"Then you don't want me?" The brazen words were out and she couldn't believe she'd actually said it.

"I wouldn't say it like that."

"Then how would you say it?"

He shook his head. "Don't look at me like that."

"How?" she asked.

"Like I yanked the funding on your project. I'm trying to be a gentleman and it's not easy."

"Why isn't it easy?"

"Oh, God—" He swallowed hard. "Because you're beautiful. The feel of you— Your skin is— So soft. You've completely destroyed the sliver of self control I've managed to retain until this second."

Her heart pounded and her spirit soared. She'd made him feel like this? "Really?"

"Hell, yes. I want you more than I've ever wanted any woman in my life."

"I want you, too." She heard his sigh of surrender and knew she'd won.

Like a gunslinger pulling a six-shooter from a holster, suddenly his card key was in his hand and a second later the door to his room was open. Flipping the switch, he led her inside as the entry lit up. The door had barely closed before she was in his arms with his mouth on hers.

Haley slid her arms around his neck and pressed against him. The muscles in her legs were going lax and she hung on for all she was worth. Marlon's kiss was filled with hunger and any insecurity she once had disappeared as instinct and need took over.

His tongue traced the seam of her lips and she gladly opened to him. When he swept inside and boldly claimed her, the tempo of her breathing increased. The moan of need in her chest refused to be contained and the sound of it fueled the tension in his body as his hands seemed to explore everywhere. He caressed her back, curved his fingers at her hips to pull her against his hardness. Sliding his palms up above her waist, he stopped and brushed his thumbs over her breasts, making her nipples erect and sensitive.

She wanted him to touch her bare skin, ached to feel her breasts in his palms. As if he could read her mind, he tugged at the hem of her T-shirt, pulling it up and over her head. With a flick of his fingers, her bra loosened and he slid the straps down her arms before dropping it on the floor.

And then he was holding her in his hands and the feeling was too wonderful. Blood pounded through her veins and between her thighs, a steady throbbing started.

"Oh, Haley," he breathed. "You're so beautiful."

She closed her eyes and drew in a shuddering breath. "That feels so good."

Such an inadequate word.

Especially when he lowered his head to her right breast and took it in his mouth. The sensation was like a jolt of sensuous electricity when he flicked his tongue over the tip. She thought the pleasure was too much to bear until he turned his attention to the left side. Unable to restrain the tension building inside her, she nearly whimpered with need.

Marlon straightened and looked at her, his eyes burning with passion. His chest was rising and falling fast and furiously. He took her hand and led her to the side of the bed.

"Are you sure about this?" he asked.

"Absolutely."

That was all he needed to hear before sweeping aside the quilt, blanket and sheet in one move. She toed off her sneakers as he unfastened the button on her jeans and slid them down with her panties. Embarrassment and shyness threatened until he dragged his shirt off. The sight of his naked chest, the contour of muscle, stole the breath from her lungs. Then he kissed her and they were skin to skin from the waist up. Shyness disappeared as the exquisite intimacy set fire to her blood.

He pulled back reluctantly and reached into his jeans' pocket for his wallet. Reaching inside with two fingers, he pulled out a square packet and set it on the nightstand. Protection. Thank goodness he'd remembered because she hardly knew her own name.

Then his heated gaze settled on her face as he unfastened his jeans and pushed them down and away. She barely had time to admire the strength of his body, the muscular arms and legs, before he easily lifted her into his arms and settled her in the center of the big bed.

Before she had a chance to get cold, he was beside her, sliding an arm beneath her and pulling her close. He cupped her cheek in his palm and kissed her. With his teeth, tongue and touch, he stoked the fire inside her. He dragged his hand over her breast and down her belly. With one finger he parted the folds of her femininity, then entered her, preparing her. His thumb brushed over the bundle of nerves coiled at the juncture of her thighs and it was like the best electrical shock she'd ever had. The jolt nearly brought her up off the bed.

But that was just the beginning. He began to stroke her—over and over—building the pressure. She writhed, unable to hold still. Her hips lifted, seeking, as the throbbing in her center grew unbearable. And then there was an explosion of pleasure like a nuclear blast. Wave after wave shuddered through her and Marlon tenderly held her until it was over.

"Oh, my God—"

He smiled. "Yeah."

Words could never describe such a feeling. Finally, she understood what all the fuss was about. Her next thought was that she didn't know it all because she was still a virgin. Before she could figure out how to phrase a question, he was reaching for the condom he'd put on the nightstand.

After covering himself, he gathered her into his arms and whispered against her hair, "You're even more passionate and responsive than I imagined."

She was stunned that he'd thought about her like this.

"You imagined me?"

"After that first kiss." He grinned. "It made me wonder. You were so quiet and shy in high school. But just that once, I felt something."

"Wow."

If only she'd known he noticed her. The revelation made her daring and she lifted a hand to his neck, then slid her fingers into the hair at his nape. Pulling him down, she settled her lips on his and felt his breathing quicken, his heart pound. He rolled over her, bracing his weight on his forearms as he nudged her thighs apart with his knee.

"Put your legs around me." There was an intensity in his husky voice, an urgency in his movements.

She did as he asked, anxious now to take the final step, know this last secret. She felt him push into her and braced herself. When he thrust gently, there was a sharp pain when the resistance was gone. But she felt him tense.

He froze for a moment, confused. "Haley?"

"Don't stop," she whispered, holding him fast. "Please."

The discomfort faded and then she wrapped her legs more securely around him, drawing him in deeper. He groaned and his hips started to move. In moments, his body went completely still, then tensed as he cried out with pleasure. She held him tight as release surged through him. Now that she knew the awesomeness of the sensation, she smiled. Her heart soared at the wonder of giving him that. When he lifted his head, she dropped her arms. He rolled out of bed, then grabbed his pants from the floor before disappearing into the bathroom.

Her body was a little sore in the best possible way and she had a flash of insight. Sex didn't make her a woman. It just made her glory in being one.

Unfortunately, the glow only lasted until Marlon came back and handed her the hotel robe that had been hanging in his closet. "We need to talk."

Not the words she'd wanted to hear. It couldn't be a good sign. "Okay."

While she slid her arms into the sleeves and tied the robe around her waist, he turned his back. But when he spoke, she didn't have to see his face to know he was upset.

"You're a virgin?"

"Not anymore." She turned on the night-stand light.

He whirled around. "Did it occur to you at any point that it was information I should have?"

"No." She leaned against the headboard. "It's kind of a catch twenty-two. I didn't know what you needed to know because I'd never done it before."

"You're twenty-four years old. How is that possible?"

"Life intervened. I got busy. And my mom always told me not to rush into sex because there's only one first time and it should be special."

He winced. "If I'd known, I would have made it special."

"It was," she protested. "I'm glad it was you. I really wanted you to be the one."

"The one?" He couldn't have looked more surprised if she'd slapped him.

"You said yourself there was something simmering between us."

"Yeah." Regret shadowed every angle of his face. "And I was stupid for saying that. I was doing my damnedest to resist temptation—"

"I'm glad you didn't." That was an attempt to tease him out of this severe mood, but the muscle jerking in his cheek told her she'd failed.

"It's no use, Haley. Maybe if I were a different man…"

"Shouldn't that be my call?"

"How can you make the right one? You have nothing to compare."

She stood up and walked over to him, close enough to feel the anger rolling off him and let him feel hers. "Sex is just a physical act. The fact that it's my first time doesn't mean I don't know my own mind. I know who I like and don't like. I've been around."

"So have I. Enough to know I'm not good enough for you. I'm not the right guy. I can't be what you need."

The words pierced her heart and drew blood. It was vital that she be alone when the pain of it hit. Without a word, she grabbed up her clothes. She'd waited to be with a man, wanting it to feel right. And it had. So wonderful, so right. And she hated that Marlon thought it was wrong.

But he was wrong. A woman who'd saved herself for the right man shouldn't feel as if she'd made a mistake.

Haley wasn't sure how she managed to find her way to the door connecting their rooms. Even more surprising was how she held back the tears. But they didn't fall until she'd made it safely to her side and was alone.

They fell because she was alone and always would be.

The next morning Haley bought a cup of coffee and a scone from the Starbucks next door to the hotel. She was steering clear of Marlon. Her eyes were swollen and achy from crying, but that wasn't the reason for her evasive actions.

What was she going to say to him about last night?

In her fantasy of first-time sex, cuddling afterward had been a component. Followed closely by falling asleep wrapped in a pair of strong arms. Her anxiety about the scenario had been more in the nature of what to do about morning breath.

Physically, she was a little sore and couldn't help being glad of the proof that she was no longer pure as the driven snow. If she'd told him, what would he have done to make it different? Most likely he'd have sent her away.

With no clear answer to the questions, she walked back to the hotel and through the Western-themed lobby. To her left was the registration desk, a replica of a saloon bar with brass foot rail. The ceiling was made of natural pine open beams and there was a river rock fireplace in the corner. A leather couch and two wing chairs formed a conversation area around it. On the coffee table stood a metal sculpture of horse and rider. Somehow the artist had managed to convey the illusion of motion, of racing across the plains.

If anyone could appreciate creativity in any medium, it was her. Sketching had always been her serenity and she figured after last night she'd be churning out a lot of stuff when she got home.

She wished she was there now and was tempted to hop in her truck and go. But she just couldn't skip out on Marlon, no matter how big a jerk he'd been. That didn't mean she wouldn't take the coward's way out and avoid him just a little while longer.

She scurried through the hotel lobby and went outside to the courtyard. Sitting on a wrought-iron bench, she scanned her surroundings. It was a landscaped rectangular area surrounded on three sides by the four-story buildings. A fenced-in pool was at the far end with grass, trees, flowers and shrubs in the middle. It was a peaceful place, or might have been if she wasn't in the middle of a personal crisis.

She should have stayed in Thunder Canyon. The trip had been a waste of time. Roy was still missing and she'd slept with her major crush. On the failure scale, she was two for two.

"Here you are."

She jumped at the sound of Marlon's voice behind her. Lost in thought and wallowing in a healthy portion of self-pity, she hadn't heard him approach.

"Here I am." She didn't turn to look at him.

"Do you mind if I join you?"

Yes. But it would be best to get this over with. She shrugged. "Suit yourself."

He sat down beside her with his own Starbucks cup in hand. "I've been looking all over for you."

"And you found me."

She dug into her bag and broke off a piece of scone—not out of hunger because her appetite had deserted her at the sound of his voice, but just for something to occupy her hands. The longer she could keep from looking at him the better.

If only she couldn't smell the spicy fragrance of his aftershave, the clean manly scent of his skin after a morning shower. Her insides quivered with excitement in spite of the rational voice warning that it was a waste of energy.

He took a sip of coffee. "Are you all right?"

"Of course." She chewed the pastry without tasting anything. "Don't I look all right?"

"That's not what I meant and you know it."

"What did you mean?"

She could have taken pity on him and answered the question she knew he was asking, but her charitable streak was nowhere to be found. If it was up to her, ignoring the whole thing would be the way to go.

He let out a long breath. "We need to talk about last night."

"No, we really don't."

"Okay then. I need to. You can just listen."

"No, I really can't." She started to stand, but his hand shot out and tugged her back down. She hated that his slightest touch put a hitch in her breathing.

"Don't be stubborn."

"Can't help it. I was made that way." She set the bag and coffee on the bench between them.

"Why didn't you tell me you'd never been with a man?"

The words felt like an accusation and she went on the defensive. "It's not something I should have to apologize for."

"God, no—" There was adamant agreement in his tone. "I'm the one who should apologize."

"Darn right." She chanced a look at him and the sincere regret in his expression deflated the serious case of mad she was carrying around. "Why?"

"I should have known," he said miserably.

That shocked her. "How could you?"

"There were signs. Your reaction to that kiss on the way to dinner, for one."

"It just surprised me. I haven't kissed that many guys." The defensive words just popped out. She prayed he wouldn't pity her. That was something she couldn't bear.

"How many?"

"A few." She glanced at him and it didn't

look like he was feeling sorry for her. "Including you? Two."

"The guy when you were in college?"

"How did you know that?"

"I asked around because—" He raked his fingers through his hair. "Your reaction when I kissed you was— I was afraid I'd screwed up. Ben and Linda didn't remember you going out with anyone in Thunder Canyon, but thought there might have been someone when you went away to school."

"You made inquiries into my personal life?"

"I was trying to understand," he defended. "I figured someone hurt you and that's why you pushed me away. Now I know the truth."

Could they just be done with this conversation? "It's no big deal."

"You're wrong. It's an incredibly big deal. When a woman gives herself to a man for the first time, it's a gift."

"Really?" Her gaze snapped up to his and she couldn't detect anything but honesty there.

"A gift and a responsibility."

"Why?"

He was quiet for several moments. "A woman's first time can affect her attitude about sex forever. A guy feels pressure to make it good. I wish I'd known—"

That was so sweet. It was the subtext of what her mom had said from the male point of view. And she knew without a doubt that her mom would have liked Marlon.

"I handled it badly," he continued. "I'm really sorry about that. Somehow I'll make it up to you."

A glow spread from her midsection outward until every part of her was tingling. Obviously he didn't consider her an alien from the planet Zatu and that boded well for a second time. She was all in favor of that.

She touched his arm and the warm skin melted any lingering insecurities. "For the record, my attitude about sex is alive and well."

He studied her for several moments, then wrapped her fingers in his big hand. Apparently he decided she was telling the truth because his mouth softened into a smile. "Good."

As much as Haley wanted to hold on to this moment, they needed to figure out their next move. "What are we going to do about Roy?"

He let go of her hand and picked up his coffee, taking a sip as he thought. "I think we've done everything we can here."

"But he's still out there somewhere."

"Billings has a population of over a hundred thousand," Marlon pointed out. "It's like looking for a needle in a haystack. There are kids in Thunder Canyon who want to hang out at ROOTS. They need to be your priority."

She sighed. "You're right. It's just—"

"The ones who run away need the most help?" he guessed.

"Yeah."

"He knows how to find you." He squeezed her fingers reassuringly, then released her and stood up. "Let's go home."

"Okay."

They walked back into the lobby and she started for the elevator when he put a hand on her arm.

"I'm going to check out at the front desk since we're down here," he said.

"I'll go with you."

They talked to Paul, the clerk on duty, who charged the credit card Marlon had given them yesterday. He'd insisted on paying for her room, too, and said she could reimburse him later. Something told her he wouldn't take her money, though.

Marlon folded the printout of the charges and slipped it into the back pocket of his jeans. "Thanks."

"No problem," the young man said. He smiled and looked at each of them in turn. "Come back and see us again, Mr. Cates. Mrs. Cates."

Haley was trying to process the fact that Paul thought they were a couple even though they'd had separate rooms. He'd probably only looked at the total, not the itemized charges. It was an honest mistake. The real surprise was Marlon's reaction.

"We're not married." His tone was adamant and he couldn't get the words out fast enough.

He could have let the misunderstanding slide. Who cared if a man they would never see again thought they were married?

Obviously Marlon cared. He'd been incredibly uncomfortable with the idea. Setting the guy straight and in that sharp tone was the equivalent of backing up several steps and putting his hands up to distance himself from any part of her being his Mrs.

It was a sad and sobering reality check. Just moments ago she'd been a starry-eyed lover looking forward to a second time. But the truth was, he regretted the first time. If she'd told him she'd never done it before, he'd have sent her to her room with a pat on the head. He didn't want the responsibility.

He didn't want to be tied down to a place or a person.

Especially a person.

And her reality check went one awful step further. This whole time she'd been worried about her crush on Marlon. Worried about making the same mistake. She wouldn't have slept with him if she didn't care. A lot. So she hadn't made the same mistake. This was so much more than a major crush.

She'd fallen in love with him.

Chapter Fourteen

It was a quiet afternoon at ROOTS. Marlon and Haley were the only ones there. They'd been back in Thunder Canyon for twenty-four hours and still no word from Roy. He hoped the kid was on her mind and not what happened between them.

Sex.

Awesome.

He still couldn't believe that she'd picked him to be her first. And if circumstances were different, if he wasn't leaving, he would show her everything he could about seduction and tenderness. But nothing had changed and something made her go distant. One minute she'd shyly told him her attitude about sex was alive and well. The next they'd checked out of the hotel and on the drive back, she got quiet and broody.

Marlon had tried more than once to draw her out. Every time he'd asked if something was bothering her she went all female on him and said everything was fine. He was beginning to hate that word.

So here they sat. Not talking. He was working on his laptop at the tiny computer desk and she was sitting behind him on the couch, with her legs tucked up beneath her and a sketch pad in her lap. The only sound in the room was her charcoal pencil scratching on the paper.

Marlon liked quiet when he worked, but the air was vibrating with tension and making him nuts. He was just about to take her on regarding the silent treatment when his phone rang.

He reached for the case on his belt and retrieved his cell. After looking at the caller ID, he smiled and answered. "Dana. How's the world's best personal assistant?"

"Crabby. When are you getting out of the slammer?" she asked.

"Technically I was never in the slammer."

"You know what I mean."

"My community service will be satisfied in about a week." So soon? When did that happen? It had gone too fast, he thought, swiveling his chair around to look at Haley. She didn't look back.

"Good. I need a vacation," Dana said.

"Because?"

"I'm running MC/TC by myself."

"I've been pulling my weight," he protested.

"Oh, please. Long distance just makes more work for me."

"I'll make it up to you when I get home."

"Don't try to get on my good side with false promises. I'm mad at you."

He leaned back in the chair and slid another quick look at Haley who was still pretending not to listen. "So the whole purpose of this call was to yell at me and make me feel guilty?"

"Of course."

"Come on, D. I know you better than that. How's business?"

"The numbers have improved slightly. Not dance-of-joy good yet, but there's reason for cautious optimism. The downward spiral has leveled off and some of the profit graphs are actually starting to go up."

"That's great news. Might be a good time to counter the buyout offer."

"So you've decided to sell?" Dana asked, disapproval leaking into her tone.

Marlon had discussed the pros and cons with her at length and knew, like Haley, she favored hanging in there. "I'm still considering all the options."

"Before you go to the dark side, consider this." He heard papers rustling. "The sketches you sent me from— What's her name?"

"Haley," he said and saw her glance up.

"Right. Haley's drawings are incredibly promising."

"I thought so."

"Boss, we could do a whole line. Love the name, by the way. A great way to brand it. HA! It's sassy and sexy."

Just like the woman herself. He glanced at Haley who was looking at him now, probably at the sound of her name and the excitement in his voice.

"That's good," he said.

"If we push it, I think we can get the product into our trial market in time for Christmas. It will be a lot of work and more up-front cost to do it. But the payoff could be really big."

"I'm glad you approve."

"You found her," Dana said. "I assume the designer is a her."

"Yes, indeed."

"She's there, isn't she?"

He met Haley's curious-but-trying-not-to-be look. "Yup."

"You can't talk?"

"I thought I was," he said.

"You know what I mean."

"Yeah. And that would be an affirmative."

"This covert conversation doesn't work for me," Dana said, going into crabby mode again. "When are you coming home?"

"I'll be back when my community service is done."

"About a week," she repeated. "Good. I'll get moving on these new designs. See you soon, boss."

"Excellent. I can't wait to see what happens." He hung up.

"Problem?" Haley didn't look distant as much as troubled.

"Actually, no." He stood and walked over to the sofa. "That was my assistant."

"I gathered. The 'world's best personal assistant' remark was a big clue."

"Dana Taylor," he confirmed. "We met in college. A business class." For some reason he felt compelled to explain. "When MC/TC started to take off, she was the first person I hired. It was a good decision."

"So everything's okay?"

"Very. She called to let me know how much she likes your designs." He waited, but there was no response. Maybe she didn't understand the potential. "She wants to try and get them in the stores by the end of the year."

Her eyes widened, but there was no excitement. "You sound anxious to get back to work."

"Dana thinks your designs will really take off. But if we're going to make it happen, there will be a lot of overtime required." He'd expected laughing, squealing, possibly dancing and hugging. What he didn't expect was no reaction at all.

She put her pad and pencil down on the table and stood. "Then I wouldn't dream of keeping you. After all the overtime here at ROOTS you've more than satisfied the court's expectations. And mine. I'll sign off on your community service right now so you can go."

Leave?

Early?

When he'd started here at ROOTS, those words would have made him pump his arm in triumph. Now? Not so much. He still had a week. He wanted that week.

"Are you trying to get rid of me?" The words were raw and angry.

The thought of leaving her was like a punch to the gut and knocked the air out of him, a lot like being tackled by a two-hundred-fifty-pound linebacker who wanted to rip his head off. Every instinct he had pushed back.

He liked Haley, everything about her.

She was beautiful. Smart. Prickly. Stubborn. Creative, sweet and funny. Pure of heart.

He liked walking into ROOTS and seeing her eyes light up at the sight of him. He liked knowing she had no idea her reaction was so obvious. Making her laugh made him happy. He especially enjoyed nudging the sad look from her eyes and wanted to make that expression disappear for good. But somehow he'd etched it even deeper and that was unacceptable.

And just like that it all became clear to him. He wanted to be in her life and to keep her in his. "Haley, I—"

"You're off the hook, Marlon. Go back to L.A." She turned and disappeared into the back room followed by the sound of the rear door opening and closing.

Marlon didn't want her to leave any more than he wanted to. It was as clear to him as the mountains around Thunder Canyon on a windy day. Maybe he should accept the offer on the table to buy his business. He could stay here. Go to work for Cates Construction. It would be great to see more of his family.

More important—he would be with Haley.

Somehow she'd gotten under his skin. All he'd ever wanted was to be a successful businessman and he'd done it. He had no idea when success had stopped being enough.

That was a lie. The seed was planted six years ago when he kissed Haley, then never followed through. Being forced to stay and work with her, his feelings had taken root and blossomed.

He had to go after her this time.

Just as he turned toward the back room where she'd disappeared, the bell over the front door clanged. Marlon did a double take when Roy Robbins strolled casually inside as if he hadn't a care in the world.

"Hey, dude—"

"Don't you dare 'hey dude' me, you pin-head."

"Haley says it's not nice to call people names."

"Well, Haley's not here right now. I am." Marlon pointed at the kid, anger rolling through him. "What the hell happened? Haley's been worried sick about you. She insisted on going all the way to Billings because you have a friend there. Obviously we didn't find you."

Marlon realized he'd found something on that trip, though.

Himself.

"Where the hell have you been?"

"Lighten up, man."

"Not a chance. I'm leaning on you hard. And you know why? You used Haley—"

"It wasn't like that," Roy protested.

"Bull. You took advantage of her good heart. Stayed at her house. Let her feed and take care of you. You used this mentoring program, one that means everything to her, as your own social network. For completely self-ish reasons. Then there's a little dust-up and you can't take the heat like a man. Gone without a word like a spoiled brat." Marlon took half a step closer. "You made Haley worry. I don't like it when she worries."

"Peace, man." Roy made a V with his index and middle fingers. "I thought it would be best for me to split."

"Best for who?"

"For Haley."

"Again I say bull. You took the chicken way out because facing her was too tough."

"She talked to me about how to man up."

"And apparently wasted her breath," Marlon accused.

Something that looked a lot like surrender flickered in the boy's eyes. And somewhere in the hazy, rational part of Marlon's mind he knew he was taking out his own frustrations on the kid. He dragged in a cleansing breath of air.

"Look, dude—" Roy caught himself and stopped. "Marlon, I didn't mean to worry her. I thought she'd be relieved if I was gone."

"You thought wrong." Some of Marlon's anger slipped away when it became clear to him that the kid regretted his actions.

"I know that now. I'll apologize to Haley before I go."

"What?"

Marlon wasn't sure whether to be surprised

or pissed off. What would Haley do in this situation? Probably bake cookies and grill Roy like raw hamburger with a touch so gentle he wouldn't realize the secrets he was giving away. Connecting to people was effortless for her. As simple as a long-ago kiss that had changed his life.

"You thirsty?" Marlon finally asked.

Roy looked wary as he nodded. "But maybe I should go find Haley—"

"That's a good idea. But it might also be a good idea to run what you're planning to say by me. I'll get a couple of sodas." Marlon pointed at him. "Stay put."

"Cool." Roy sat on the couch.

When he came back with the drinks, the kid hadn't moved. He handed Roy a cold can, then sat in the worn chair beside him and popped the tab on his own soda.

"So we know why you took off from Thunder Canyon. Where did you go?"

"Helena." Roy lifted the tab on his drink and took a long swallow of the cold liquid.

Helena? What the heck?

"Why there?" Marlon asked calmly.

"It's where my cousin lives."

"So when you ran away from home, why

didn't you go to your cousin's in the first place instead of Thunder Canyon?"

"He'd have ratted me out to my folks and I didn't plan to go home ever again. Then," he added.

"Do you want to talk about it?"

"Not really." A small smile curved the corners of his mouth. "But Haley says talking is a good way to sort things out."

"You should listen to her," Marlon advised.

Roy nodded. "There was this girl—Whitney."

"A woman. Why doesn't that surprise me?" He took a drink of his soda to stop any more editorial comments from slipping out. Not helpful, Haley would have said. "Go on."

"She's a cheerleader. A real fox. Extremely hot." Roy met his gaze to see if his meaning sank in.

"I'm old, but the teenage boy/cheerleader fantasy is an unforgettable classic for guys of all ages," Marlon explained wryly.

Roy grinned, but it faded a moment later. "She dumped me. It was on her Facebook page. The whole school was tweeting about it."

"It happens."

"But, dude, I never saw it coming. We were

voted the couple most likely to last until graduation." Roy's eyes were full of teenage tragedy. "And she didn't even give me a reason. She said I didn't do anything, but the relationship just ran its course and we were over."

"That's rough." Marlon sincerely meant that.

"Everyone knew. I just couldn't stick around. The pity was a total drag."

"I can see where you'd feel that way." And this was the part Marlon really wanted to talk about. "But Haley will be upset if you take off again."

"It's not taking off." Roy looked up. "I'm going home. My mom is on her way. I just came back to thank Haley for everything she did for me. I don't know how I'll ever repay her for—"

"Thanks will be enough. She doesn't want anything but for you to be okay." Marlon reached over and squeezed the kid's shoulder approvingly. "You gonna be okay? When you get home? Maybe you could talk to Whitney."

Roy nodded thoughtfully. "I'd sure like to know why she dumped me. To understand what was going through her mind."

Good luck with that, Marlon thought. Fortunately the words didn't come out of his mouth. "Talking is good. Just don't forget that the female mind is a dark and complicated place."

"Dude, you're talking about Haley, aren't you?"

"That's a pretty big leap." It was true, Marlon thought, but still a big leap.

"You didn't deny it, so I must be right." Roy pointed at him. "You like her."

"Of course I do. Everyone in town likes her."

"That's what Haley said when I asked her about you."

"What?" Marlon asked.

"You want to hook up with Haley. A blind man could see that."

No way was he telling this kid that they'd already hooked up and all it accomplished was to make everything even more complicated. "It's not that simple."

"Why do adults always say that about their relationships? Do you think for us kids it's a day at the beach?"

"You have a point," Marlon admitted.

"I know Haley likes you."

"Really? Did she say so?"

What was this? Junior high? Should he pass her a note in study hall?

"Not exactly." Roy shrugged. "But when I called her on it, she said the same thing you just did. That she likes everyone. It was an answer, but not really. You know what I mean? Like you just now. And it was the way she said it, also just like you."

Haley liked him? Of course she did. She'd gone to bed with him. She'd chosen him to be her first. That filled him with pride followed closely by humility. But did it mean that they had a chance for something real and lasting? Was she the one?

"Look, dude, you can't run away. Reaching a milestone age doesn't make you a man. It's staying put and dealing with stuff that does it."

Marlon suppressed a smile. The kid wasn't so much a pinhead any more. He'd recently acquired some wisdom and was paying it forward. Following Haley's example. When they'd played one-on-one basketball, Marlon had taken him down a peg or two. Maybe it was time to hand back his ego.

Marlon heard the back door open and close just as he said, "What do you suggest I do?"

"You like Haley, right?"

"Yeah."

Roy nodded with smug satisfaction about

guessing correctly. "You gotta tell her how much you care."

There was a small sound behind them and Marlon turned.

Haley stood in the doorway. "You care about me?"

Chapter Fifteen

Haley wanted to take back the question. If Marlon added that he cared about her "as a friend", the humiliation would be so much worse than not knowing how to kiss.

And then it sank in that he was talking to Roy, and relief flooded her. "You're okay," she said to the teen.

"I was with my cousin." He was standing between the old sofa and coffee table. "I didn't mean to make you worry. Or cause trouble with your family. Marlon said you looked for me in Billings."

"You said something about a friend there." And if she hadn't eavesdropped, none of what happened in Billings would have happened.

It hurt a lot that Marlon's heated protest at being mistaken as part of a couple confirmed that he was a contented bachelor. But she would never be sorry he'd made love to her. It was a memory she would hold close to her forever.

"Say something, Haley," Roy begged.

She smiled. "Next time leave a note."

"I thought it would be best to just go, that it would be better for you."

"I appreciate your concern, really. But there was no need to disappear." She moved farther into the room, keeping the sofa between her and the two guys. "There is something we need to talk about, though. You know I care about you, but sooner or later you have to go home."

"Done."

She blinked at him. "Really?"

"I called my mom. She's on her way and was pretty cool on the phone. Said we have to talk about stuff, but it can wait till we get home."

Haley was happy for him. "No threats of grounding for the rest of your life?"

"Not yet. But I'm sure there will be consequences," the teen said ruefully.

"I hope so. It means they care."

"Then the state of Montana cares big time about Marlon," Roy joked, glancing at the man in question. "What with his community service consequences."

Haley didn't even want to peek at him. It was hard enough hanging on to her composure when she pretended he wasn't there. But looking at him with all his masculinity, magnetism and charisma, not to mention charm, broke her heart just a little more every time.

"The state of Montana doesn't give a rat's behind about me. It's all about rules to keep civilization civilized." Marlon's voice was laced with humor but underneath it had an edge.

Haley could feel his gaze and her skin grew warm as her heart beat too fast. "I'm glad you're working things out with your family."

"It was a girl," Roy said.

"What?" She was confused at the sudden change of topic.

"The reason I ran away. She dumped me and wouldn't say why. I didn't want to face anyone. My parents blew me off. Said everyone goes through it and we all have to learn to live with disappointment. They didn't understand." Roy folded his arms over his chest. "But running away was immature. I'm going to talk to Whitney about it when I get home."

"Very grown-up decision."

"Marlon mentioned that it might be a good idea."

It was. Darn him. She wanted him to be a jerk so she could elevate her anger to a certain level and keep out the pain. He was taking that away from her, too.

"When's your mom coming?"

"Not long," Roy answered. "I wanted to tell you first. Then I need to say goodbye to C.J. and the others before I go."

Haley nodded her approval. "Good plan."

He hesitated for a moment. "Would it be okay if I gave you a hug? I mean, Austin's not going to break down the door and beat me up or anything, is he?"

"He's at work. The coast is clear." She opened her arms and he walked around the sofa into them.

"Thanks, Haley. For everything. Seriously."

"You're welcome." Her throat was thick with emotion and her feelings were mixed. She was incredibly glad the program she'd started had helped him, but would miss him terribly. "You're part of the family, kiddo. Don't be a stranger."

"No way." He shook hands with Marlon, then walked out the door.

Through the big window she saw him look back and grin. He waved once and was gone. Now she was alone with Marlon and the question she'd asked just a few minutes before. Maybe he hadn't heard or didn't remember.

He looked at her. "I do care about you, Haley."

Heard and remembered, she thought.

"That's nice of you to say."

"Nice has nothing to do with anything. It just is."

He didn't sound happy about that, but join the club. She wasn't happy about her feelings either. "Anyway, thanks for all your help."

There was an angry expression in his dark eyes when he rounded the sofa and stood in front of her. "What are you doing?"

"Saying goodbye." It was a miracle that she kept her voice from cracking. She couldn't show any weakness that would betray the raging emotions churning inside.

"I'm not going anywhere."

"Your community service is complete."

"Signing off on it early doesn't mean you're getting rid of me."

"News flash, Marlon, you don't live here anymore."

"About that—" He rubbed a hand across the back of his neck. "I'm seriously considering taking the buyout offer for my company."

And completely sever any ties he had to this town? Every part of her protested and she wondered if it was about losing even that small connection to him.

"But your business was born in Thunder Canyon," she argued. "You'd be putting your dream in someone else's hands. Like giving your baby away."

"Some things are more important than business."

"Like what?"

"You." Intensity burned in his eyes.

"I don't understand." Her heart was hammering and blood roared in her ears. She couldn't possibly have heard him right.

"I'm thinking about going to work in the family construction business. Permanently settling in Thunder Canyon."

For her? She wasn't the sort of woman that a man gave everything up for. That just wasn't possible. She wasn't a woman who could be played with, either.

"Look, Marlon, I'm not sure where this is coming from. It's out of character for you."

"I think I know my own character pretty well, so I'm confused about your reaction." His eyes narrowed on her.

"Then let me explain. When you checked out of the hotel in Billings the clerk called us Mr. and Mrs. Cates. Just the misunderstanding made you start to sweat. The words were barely out of his mouth and you were jumping down his throat, correcting him. That shows pretty clearly how much commitment is still not one of your strengths." Her chin lifted. "So, I'm not sure what's going on with you, but don't expect me to fall into your arms. I don't want to be someone you settle for."

A multitude of emotions rolled through his eyes like thunderheads until anger locked into place. "I suppose I should have expected that from the status quo queen."

She winced at the ice in his tone. "Excuse me?"

"You have an exciting opportunity, Haley. The chance to design a line of products for my company, a major national brand. It's a chance to achieve your dream. But were you excited?" He shook his head. "I didn't see it."

"Because there's a lot to consider. How can I leave my family? They count on me. And ROOTS? Who would keep it going? It's an important program." She sucked in a deep breath. "Thunder Canyon is my home."

"You didn't even discuss options. A move away might not be necessary and Thunder Canyon is just geography. Home is where you make it. And if you think staying here is about community loyalty, you're not just lying to me this time. You're lying to yourself."

"Who do you think you are?" she said angrily.

"The guy who's keeping it real. You're a coward, Haley Anderson." He pointed at her to underline his words. "You call it noble and everyone here thinks you have wings and a halo. But the truth is you're afraid to leave."

Marlon turned and his broad back was the last thing she saw before he slammed the door. His accusations ricocheted around the empty room, stirring up a host of painful memories.

She'd been brave once. She'd left Thunder Canyon and life as she'd known it came crashing down around her.

It was going to happen again even though she wasn't the one leaving. This time Marlon was and he'd be taking her heart with him.

This time she would never be whole again.

Nell Anderson—Beloved Mother.

Haley's eyes filled with tears and her throat was thick with emotion as she stared at the headstone in Thunder Canyon cemetery. Feelings welled up that were about losing Marlon and not the loss she'd suffered so many years ago.

Beloved Mother.

The words were deceptively simple.

"I do love you, Mom. And I miss you now more than ever," she whispered. "I could sure use someone to talk to."

The sun was shining in a cloudless blue sky. A perfect Montana day. She set the bright bouquet of yellow daisies, purple mums and baby's breath on the grass. "I'm in love with Marlon Cates. Can you believe it? Sensible, practical me and Thunder Canyon's legendary bad boy?"

A sudden gust of wind swirled around her as if Mother Nature was responding to a disclosure that turned the universe on its ear. It had definitely taken Haley by surprise.

On the road behind her she heard a car door close. She felt more than heard footsteps on the grassy ground and the hair at her nape prickled with awareness. Somehow she knew it was the bad boy in question.

"Haley?"

Her heart was beating too fast when she met Marlon's gaze. It had been a couple of days since she'd seen him. Worn jeans fit his muscular legs as if they were tailor-made for him. A black T-shirt hugged his wide chest and aviator sunglasses hid his eyes. He looked every inch worthy of his reputation, but now she knew it was nothing more than a façade. His heart was good.

"What are you doing here?" she asked.

"I wanted to see you."

"How did you find me?"

"Ben." He took off the glasses and hung them from the neck of his shirt and moved to stand beside her, their arms nearly brushing. "He told me you come here almost every Sunday to put flowers on your mother's grave."

"I do." She looked down. "I guess the court reinstated your driver's license."

"I'm legal again. Got my wheels back," he confirmed.

"And this joyride to the cemetery is to celebrate?"

"Not exactly. I needed to talk to you."

He was leaving; she could hear it in his voice. The realization was like a physical blow. It knocked the wind out of her and hurt clear through to her soul. She desperately wanted to curl into the fetal position and fold in on herself to keep the pain from spreading, but dignity trumped weakness.

"You didn't have to come all this way outside of town to say goodbye."

"I didn't." He looked sheepish. And too cute for words. "I mean, I did. I'm here. But not to say goodbye."

Haley was confused. He had a license to leave. Why was he making this harder? "What did you want to talk about?"

"I wanted to tell you that I love you, Haley. I'm in love with you."

The direct statement knocked the wind out of her and felt like a punch to the gut, but there was no pain. Shock and awe, yes, just before disbelief crept in. "Is this some kind of joke?"

"Look, I know you're ticked off about how I handled that situation at the hotel in Billings." He looked down. "It was a knee-jerk reaction. Jerk being the operative word. I was still processing the fact that you'd never been with a man before and chose me to be the one. Mostly I was dealing with not deserving you."

"So you're here out of a sense of responsibility?" She folded her arms over her chest. "No, thanks. I can take care of myself."

"Of course you can. That's not—" He raked his fingers through his hair. "I'm really messing this up. In my own defense, let me say that I've only recently acquired any experience talking about feelings."

"I don't get it."

"Roy and I discussed his reaction to getting dumped by a girl. My comments were sensitive and reasonable."

"You're the expert on the male point of view," she said wryly.

"And in the past I'd have just taken him out for a beer and called it a day."

"He's not old enough to drink."

"You know what I mean. I didn't blow off his feelings. Because now I know what love feels like. Thanks to you."

Haley studied his expression. She'd gotten to know him really well and knew when he was teasing or when something bothered him. She could tell when he was angry, annoyed or getting his stubborn on. She was absolutely certain that he was telling her the truth.

"You really do love me."

"Finally," he said grinning. "I didn't have to work that hard to convince a venture capitalist to invest in my company." He curved his fingers around her upper arms, then pulled her close. "And you're in love with me, too."

Liquid heat poured through her and pooled in her belly when he touched his lips to hers. She sighed and sank into him, every nerve ending in her body doing the happy dance. Until reality set in.

Haley pulled away. "It doesn't matter how I feel because you're leaving."

"Says who?" When she opened her mouth to answer, he touched a finger to her lips. "You're wrong, Haley. Staying in Thunder Canyon wouldn't be settling. Not if you were with me—" He hesitated, then intensity darkened his eyes. "If you were my wife, anywhere we were together would be home. It's where the heart is and you have mine. I've traveled a lot but I've never met anyone who made me want to stay. Not until you. The most beautiful woman, inside and out, was right in my own backyard."

"Really?"

He nodded. "You gave me back my roots."

She glanced beside her, to her mother's final resting place. As the word sank in she remembered the sampler. "There are but two lasting bequests we can give our children—roots and wings," she whispered.

"Amen."

She looked up. "You're right about me, Marlon. I'm a lying coward and I don't see how you could love me."

"What?"

"I fibbed about not remembering that kiss at the football fundraiser. And I felt what was going on between us that very first day when you walked into ROOTS. It was easier to pretend not to care."

"Why?"

"Because I'm afraid of change, afraid to go." The breeze blew a strand of hair into her eyes and she pushed it away. "The last time I left—the only time—I lost the most important person in my life. Everything turned upside down."

"I know, sweetheart." He reached a hand out, but she backed away. "Okay, I'm going to say something that you already know because you told me that night at dinner in Billings. But it's the truth and I'll keep repeating the words until the message finally sinks in."

"What?" she asked when he hesitated.

"Bad stuff happens. No one can control it. Not you, or me, or anyone. Losing your mom was the worst. But it had nothing to do with the fact that you weren't here. You didn't cause the accident just because you went away."

His gaze was magnetic, willing what he said to sink in. And finally she allowed it through. All these years she'd been winging it, telling herself that's what the wings part of roots and wings meant. Now she realized her mom's lasting legacy was to not be afraid to take flight. To follow her dream wherever it took her.

Now she could let herself see that her dream was Marlon.

The weight Haley had been carrying lifted from her shoulders. Or maybe her burden felt lighter because there was another, stronger, pair of shoulders to share it.

"You're right. So right." Haley walked into his arms and rested her cheek on his chest. "I love you, Marlon. If what you said was an actual proposal, I would love to marry you."

"I'm going to hold you to that," he said fervently. "I'll spend the rest of my life proving to you that commitment is one of my strengths."

"I was wrong about that. You do commitment pretty darn well." A warm feeling slid down her spine that felt a lot like the comforting touch of her mother's hand. In her heart, Haley knew it was her mother's approval of this man, their marriage. She looked up at him and smiled. "My mother gave me roots and you fixed my broken wings. I'll follow you anywhere."

Epilogue

Haley had been afraid no one would come to the grand opening of ROOTS and had never been happier to be wrong. A week after she'd accepted Marlon's proposal, she'd managed to get everything here. Her mother's sampler was hanging on the wall with a commemorative plaque dedicating the Nell Anderson ROOTS Teen Center to her memory.

She and Marlon looked around the crowded storefront-turned-teen center where a good portion of the Thunder Canyon community was helping themselves to cookies, brownies, coffee and punch. He hugged her, pride in his eyes. "It's certainly an impressive turnout."

A lot of faces she knew. One she'd just met. Dillon Traub. He was the good-looking doctor filling in for Marlon's brother Marshall, who was taking a delayed honeymoon trip with his wife, Mia.

She leaned into Marlon and said, "I love you."

"Of course you do." The familiar twinkle gleamed in his eyes when he looked at her.

Marlon's twin, Matt, moved beside them. "Rumor has it that you're turning down the buyout offer on the company, bro."

"Not a rumor. Fact." He smiled proudly at her. "I'm recruiting some new designing talent to breathe life into it. We're tightening the belt to ride out the tough economic times. Then we'll be poised to kick some serious retail butt. Did I mention that I plan to marry the talent and make sure I've got her locked in for life?"

Matt nodded. "You two look happy."

"There's a good reason for that." Haley felt all aglow, even if no one could tell and her feet hadn't touched the ground for a week. "Marlon's taking me to Hawaii. He wants my first time seeing the ocean to be in paradise."

Marlon shot a warning look at his brother. "Don't you dare say it."

"You mean I told you so?" Matt grinned.

"What did you tell him?" Haley demanded.

"That you might be The One."

"Well, he's the one for me," she said. "But not because of Hawaii. If he took me to a laundromat, I'd still be the happiest, luckiest girl on the planet."

"Don't you have a speech to give?" Marlon asked, before his twin could rib him unmercifully.

"Yes, I do. But it's so loud in here, I'm not sure how to get everyone to listen."

Marlon guided her to the far end of the room and then put his fingers to his lips. The next sound out of him was an earsplitting whistle. Conversation stopped and everyone looked at them.

"Attention, everyone," he said. "Haley has something to say."

She smiled her appreciation, then nervously cleared her throat. "Thanks for coming. This is an awesome turnout. A lot of you know this program has been a dream of mine ever since my mom died. Without the help of the people here in Thunder Canyon, my brother, sister and I wouldn't have made it through that awful time. This center is my way of saying thank-you."

She looked out at the smiling faces. Ben Walters was there with Linda Powell beside him. Marlon's folks, Frank and Edie Cates, nodded approvingly. They'd given a big thumbs up to her engagement to their son. Austin and Angie were clapping. The two of them had been in touch with Roy, who, it turned out, didn't live far away. He'd started his senior year and was doing great.

She looked up at Marlon, who smiled his encouragement. Turning back at the crowd, she said, "I have some good news and bad. Some of you already know, but for those who don't, Marlon Cates and I are going to be married."

The announcement was greeted by applause, whistles and cheers. She held up her left hand and wiggled the ring finger with the breathtaking diamond. Just the night before Marlon had gone down on one knee and formally popped the question, then sealed the deal with the impressive jewelry.

"The thing is," she continued, "I'm moving to Los Angeles and that means I have to step down as the director of ROOTS." When the crowd made noises of disappointment, she held up her hands. "I appreciate that. You'll never know how much. But the center will continue to operate with a dedicated staff of volunteers. My brother, Austin, promised to put in some time before he goes to graduate school, courtesy of the Marlon Cates scholarship fund." Her future husband wouldn't take no for an answer on that front. "My sister, Angie, will also put in some hours. So will Linda Powell and Ben Walters—" When she looked at the older man, he pointed to Marlon and gave her a nod of endorsement. She took a deep breath. "And last but definitely not least, Carleigh Benedict of Thunder Canyon Social Services is going to take over as director. She was my adviser, mentor and friend, and the kids will be lucky to have her. Please give her your legendary Thunder Canyon support."

The pretty blonde waved and smiled when the crowd clapped enthusiastically.

"That's the spirit," Haley said. "In conclusion, I'd like to say that donations to the program are always gratefully accepted. It's sad to say goodbye, but Marlon and I will visit all the time. ROOTS is in very good hands."

And so am I, she thought as her Montana millionaire pulled her into his arms.

* * * * *

YES! Please send me **The Montana Mavericks Collection** in Larger Print. This collection begins with 3 FREE books and 2 FREE gifts (gifts valued at approx. $20.00 retail) in the first shipment, along with the other first 4 books from the collection! If I do not cancel, I will receive 8 monthly shipments until I have the entire 51-book Montana Mavericks collection. I will receive 2 or 3 FREE books in each shipment and I will pay just $4.99 US/ $5.89 CDN for each of the other four books in each shipment, plus $2.99 for shipping and handling per shipment.*If I decide to keep the entire collection, I'll have paid for only 32 books, because 19 books are FREE! I understand that accepting the 3 free books and gifts places me under no obligation to buy anything. I can always return a shipment and cancel at any time. My free books and gifts are mine to keep no matter what I decide.

263 HCN 2404   463 HCN 2404

Name	(PLEASE PRINT)	

Address		Apt. #

City	State/Prov.	Zip/Postal Code

Signature (if under 18, a parent or guardian must sign)

Mail to the **Reader Service**:
IN U.S.A.: P.O. Box 1867, Buffalo, NY 14240-1867
IN CANADA: P.O. Box 609, Fort Erie, Ontario L2A 5X3

REQUEST YOUR FREE BOOKS!

2 FREE NOVELS PLUS 2 FREE GIFTS!

⊕HARLEQUIN®

SPECIAL EDITION

Life, Love & Family

YES! Please send me 2 FREE Harlequin® Special Edition novels and my 2 FREE gifts (gifts are worth about $10). After receiving them, if I don't wish to receive any more books, I can return the shipping statement marked "cancel." If I don't cancel, I will receive 6 brand-new novels every month and be billed just $4.74 per book in the U.S. or $5.24 per book in Canada. That's a savings of at least 14% off the cover price! It's quite a bargain! Shipping and handling is just 50¢ per book in the U.S. and 75¢ per book in Canada.* I understand that accepting the 2 free books and gifts places me under no obligation to buy anything. I can always return a shipment and cancel at any time. Even if I never buy another book, the two free books and gifts are mine to keep forever.

235/335 HDN F46C

Name	(PLEASE PRINT)
Address	Apt. #
City	State/Prov.	Zip/Postal Code

Signature (if under 18, a parent or guardian must sign)

Mail to the Harlequin® Reader Service:
IN U.S.A.: P.O. Box 1867, Buffalo, NY 14240-1867
IN CANADA: P.O. Box 609, Fort Erie, Ontario L2A 5X3

Want to try two free books from another line?
Call 1-800-873-8635 or visit www.ReaderService.com.

* Terms and prices subject to change without notice. Prices do not include applicable taxes. Sales tax applicable in N.Y. Canadian residents will be charged applicable taxes. Offer not valid in Quebec. This offer is limited to one order per household. Not valid for current subscribers to Harlequin Special Edition books. All orders subject to credit approval. Credit or debit balances in a customer's account(s) may be offset by any other outstanding balance owed by or to the customer. Please allow 4 to 6 weeks for delivery. Offer available while quantities last.

Your Privacy—The Harlequin® Reader Service is committed to protecting your privacy. Our Privacy Policy is available online at www.ReaderService.com or upon request from the Harlequin Reader Service.

We make a portion of our mailing list available to reputable third parties that offer products we believe may interest you. If you prefer that we not exchange your name with third parties, or if you wish to clarify or modify your communication preferences, please visit us at www.ReaderService.com/consumerschoice or write to us at Harlequin Reader Service Preference Service, P.O. Box 9062, Buffalo, NY 14269. Include your complete name and address.

HSEDIR13R

REQUEST YOUR FREE BOOKS!
2 FREE NOVELS PLUS 2 FREE GIFTS!

HARLEQUIN
American ★ Romance®
LOVE, HOME & HAPPINESS

YES! Please send me 2 FREE Harlequin® American Romance® novels and my 2 FREE gifts (gifts are worth about $10). After receiving them, if I don't wish to receive any more books, I can return the shipping statement marked "cancel." If I don't cancel, I will receive 4 brand-new novels every month and be billed just $4.74 per book in the U.S. or $5.24 per book in Canada. That's a savings of at least 14% off the cover price! It's quite a bargain! Shipping and handling is just 50¢ per book in the U.S. and 75¢ per book in Canada.* I understand that accepting the 2 free books and gifts places me under no obligation to buy anything. I can always return a shipment and cancel at any time. Even if I never buy another book, the two free books and gifts are mine to keep forever.

154/354 HDN F4YY

Name _____ (PLEASE PRINT)

Address _____ Apt. #

City _____ State/Prov. _____ Zip/Postal Code

Signature (if under 18, a parent or guardian must sign)

Mail to the **Harlequin®** Reader Service:
IN U.S.A.: P.O. Box 1867, Buffalo, NY 14240-1867
IN CANADA: P.O. Box 609, Fort Erie, Ontario L2A 5X3

Want to try two free books from another line?
Call 1-800-873-8635 or visit www.ReaderService.com.

* Terms and prices subject to change without notice. Prices do not include applicable taxes. Sales tax applicable in N.Y. Canadian residents will be charged applicable taxes. Offer not valid in Quebec. This offer is limited to one order per household. Not valid for current subscribers to Harlequin American Romance books. All orders subject to credit approval. Credit or debit balances in a customer's account(s) may be offset by any other outstanding balance owed by or to the customer. Please allow 4 to 6 weeks for delivery. Offer available while quantities last.

Your Privacy—The Harlequin® Reader Service is committed to protecting your privacy. Our Privacy Policy is available online at www.ReaderService.com or upon request from the Harlequin Reader Service.

We make a portion of our mailing list available to reputable third parties that offer products we believe may interest you. If you prefer that we not exchange your name with third parties, or if you wish to clarify or modify your communication preferences, please visit us at www.ReaderService.com/consumerchoice or write to us at Harlequin Reader Service Preference Service, P.O. Box 9062, Buffalo, NY 14269. Include your complete name and address.

HARDIR13R